The Valdepeñas

THE VALDEPEÑAS

by

Richard Lortz

'The head Sublime, the heart
Pathos, the genitals Beauty, the
hands and feet Proportion.'
William Blake

1980

Second Chance Press

Sagaponack, NY

Library of Congress Catalogue Card Number 79-66114
International Standard Book Numbers:
Clothbound 0-933256-06-X
Paperbound 0-933256-07-8

First published in 1961 by Peter Davies, London
under the title: *A Summer in Spain*

Manufactured in the United States of America

SECOND CHANCE PRESS, INC.
Sagaponack, NY 11962

Part One

I

THE young Italian actress had nodded to Mrs Wainwright Carter several times: once in the dining salon, twice as they passed each other in the hotel lobby. And now, not unexpectedly, she sat herself down on the beach beside the older woman and began smoothing suntan lotion into her skin and speaking about the climate, and the sea, and how charming Corbodéra was – and how wretched the hotel.

'My toilet wheezes and groans if I so much as *look* at it,' she said. 'But I do not mind; not really. I am used to bad plumbing. I am used to *no* plumbing. I was very poor as a child. Nothing disconcerts me. If necessary, I could go to the bathroom in the sea.'

'The hotel is *mine*,' Mrs Carter informed her. Her accent was British, slight but unmistakable. 'I bought it several years ago, but even the management doesn't know, though I do believe it suspects.'

It was an intimacy – so like Mrs Carter – that solicited immediate loyalty, instant secrecy. The actress was surprised, not at all embarrassed at her *faux pas*, and looked with new interest at her companion.

'My agent arranged my stay here,' she said. 'I have just finished a picture in Rome, and I am exhausted. "No crowds," I told him; "no people at all. Somewhere quiet, secluded, *isolated* if possible; *away* from the Continent. Not France, and certainly not Italy. Spain, perhaps. An island off the coast. Some place *no* one has ever heard of."'

'– So he found you Corbodéra,' Mrs Carter smiled; 'and the Polonaise.'

3

A fly had bitten the actress; with an oath she brushed it from her leg.

'It is a strange name for a Spanish hotel.'

'Yes,' Mrs Carter agreed. 'It was called that when I bought it and I never thought to change. Nor have I modernised it in any way, as you have observed. I am not interested in attracting guests; indeed, my trouble is keeping them away. The Polonaise is simply a summer place. I am here only two months of the year with a few of my friends, and I do not invite them particularly; they come and go, and sometimes someone new and interesting turns up – like yourself, perhaps – and I am content to be with whomever I find, or whoever finds me.'

The flies were particularly troublesome this morning. They were the *geistata*, the large green variety with the tiny horned heads and mean eyes. They were peculiar to Corbodéra; at least Mrs Carter had never encountered them elsewhere.

'They are here for only two weeks,' she said, referring to the insects and feeling some word of apology necessary. The *geistata* were always intensely disliked, but less so if one knew something of their history and habits. 'After that, they disappear into the chalk cliffs where they build strange geodesic houses, mixing various body enzymes with the chalk which they chew up in their mouths.'

The actress didn't seem particularly impressed, but Mrs Carter went on undiscouraged.

' – In each house they leave a tiny hole, presumably for ventilation or to maintain a certain precise temperature. Insects are very fussy, you know.' She paused, but there was no comment. '– I have looked into their houses once or twice – you can see them when the sun is just right – but the most I ever discovered was a pair of beady green eyes staring back at me, as mean, it seemed, as ever.'

4

She brushed one from her arm, adding: 'Then, in a day or two, all the little holes are cemented up. I can't imagine what happens after that. I often thought I could crack one open if I brought a hammer with me – just to see, you know. But then – I am not sure I really *want* to know what goes on. The insect world is so inhuman.'

The actress remained unimpressed, the fascinating habits of the *geistata* apparently in no way alleviating the pain of their sharp stings.

She kept tossing on her blanket, now sitting up, now lying down, repeating a string of harsh Italian words.

'I have observed,' Mrs Carter said presently, 'that if you can manage to kill a few, and then arrange the corpses on the sand next to you with their little legs sticking up, the others are *convinced* of the depth of your animosity and leave you alone.'

The actress laughed.

'I shall try it,' she said, and rolled up her movie magazine for a swatter. In no time she had killed five.

'You have a very steady eye,' Mrs Carter observed, watching her closely; 'and a quick hand. That is a good sign. I suppose it comes from being an actress and having to remember all those lines – when to speak and when to smile and not to smile. I could never do that. I was once in a movie I am told, though I never saw it personally. A little fat man from Hollywood made a picture here – or tried to – right where you are sitting, or a little way beyond.' She paused, her eyes peering intently over the tops of her sunglasses, as if it were important to remember the exact spot. 'I never knew how he got to the island; he must have had private means. In any event, he had artificial palm trees with him – it was a picture about the south seas – and while he was strewing them along the beach the bellboy came and told me. I was outraged, of course, when I looked from my window and saw all that green crêpe paper floating in the wind. I rushed down with my hotel agent who happened to be here at the time and literally *ordered* the whole company to another part of the island. They went, of course. And I noticed that the palm trees folded. They were collapsible!'

The actress seemed in no way surprised, but then, she was part of the film industry and probably knew all about many of its astonishing deceptions.

'The point of what I am saying, however,' Mrs Carter continued, 'is that all the cameras were working when I came along the beach with my agent. Some sort of crowd scene was going on, with the natives milling about, all painted up to resemble Polynesians. And there we were – completely civilised! – I in my *contura*, and my agent in a white straw hat!' She laughed, adding: 'I am told that because of the budget we were left in the film – and made out to be English missionaries who had come to convert the natives but were thwarted. Isn't that interesting?'

'I have never heard anything more interesting,' the young actress replied, smiling. 'But how is it you did not *see* the film? I would have been curious.'

'Well, I admit I was,' Mrs Carter confessed. 'And it did play in Barcelona the following year. There is an American Film Festival there, you know, with Spanish titles. But . . . I don't know. I am lazy once I settle here for the summer. And the others had already arrived. Mildred had been sea-sick as usual, poor dear. And it takes days for her to recover. There is something wrong with the labyrinth in one of her inner ears. The fluid isn't of the proper consistency – some such thing. Why once' – Mrs Carter pointed to the sea – 'once she was floating out there on a rubber mattress, the kind you fill with air – and became so violently ill she couldn't raise a hand to paddle to shore, or even call out. There she was – floating out and out – like a dead Ophelia – or that barge, what is that barge in King Arthur where everyone is always floating down the river? Lorraine – or Elaine! – isn't that the name? "Elaine, the fair, Elaine, the lovable . . ." Well, poor Mildred would have floated away for ever, if it hadn't been for Robert. He's our "writer"– and has very keen eyes, you know, and he noticed how far the mattress had gone. Why it seemed just a speck on the horizon! Naturally we rescued her. But she was positively *green* when we got her to shore. Never have I seen such a colour! Except – yes, once when I was in Moscow, a young ballerina was stricken on the stage. I believe, that time, it was ptomaine. . . .'

2

BEHIND her, on the pavilion, a flash of white caught Mrs Carter's eye.

'Don't look now,' she said to the actress, 'but when you get a chance, peek over your shoulder. There is a young man standing on one of the balconies. . . .'

The actress pretended to swat a fly and at the same time glanced back.

'That is the *American* who arrived yesterday,' Mrs Carter whispered. ' – Just a few hours before you did. He's a doctor, a psychiatrist, and he has a very lovely French wife. Doesn't it make your heart ache?'

'I have never been married,' the actress replied. 'I doubt that I ever shall be.'

'Nonsense,' Mrs Carter reproved. 'You are very young. You shall have many husbands.'

'No——' the actress shook her head. The flies seemed less bothersome now, and she lay inert on her blanket, every pore of her body welcoming the intense heat of the sun. 'I don't like men. Which is not to imply that I like women – *that* way . . . Though I will admit that I loved a girl when I was fourteen. But what is that? Every girl loves a girl when she is fourteen. It is the way we get *used* to men, to someone other than ourselves touching and loving. Since then I have had several male lovers. One must do *something*. Otherwise there is insomnia and short temper. But marriage?——' She shrugged. 'My mother had seventeen children. I was the first. – Even now, with all the money I have given them, they are screaming and fighting back in Rome.' Again she shook her head, but this time with a sound like a laugh. 'No,' she concluded, 'no – there is nothing a child can say, no matter how wicked, no matter how charming, that I have not heard. There is nothing a child can *do* that I haven't seen a thousand times. So – I shall never have children. There have been too many in my life already. And therefore I shall never marry. What is the point?'

'That is a very *young* philosophy,' Mrs Carter observed gently. 'Perhaps, when you are older . . .'

'When one is young,' the actress interrupted, brushing a fly from her nose, 'one has young lovers. When one is old, one still has young lovers. Rome is filled with hungry boys. Buy one a new suit or a pair of shiny shoes and he is your slave. And if a boy will not do – well, an old lover, if he is not fat, is not so bad. They have talents the young never dreamed of. They will cook your breakfast, and fan you when the weather is hot.'

Mrs Carter laughed. The actress's frankness and simplicity delighted her.

She glanced back at the hotel, at the ornate pink and white structure, the absurd garlands of stone flowers with which some insane architect had festooned its façade as well as every window, every door, every balcony that faced the sea. Truly there was something strange about the Polonaise. There was nothing she had to do – simply sit here, simply wait each summer for people as stimulating as the actress to be drawn to her side. This summer – and it was still so early – was promising to be more exciting than any other. The Countess was sure to return – after the *geistata* had flown to the chalk cliffs – and bring someone unusual and interesting with her. She was never alone. And Robert would arrive soon, too. Mildred Hawkins was already there – groaning on her bed in Suite

204. Mrs Carter had fed her camomile tea, spooning it to her mouth, but nothing helped really. The poor dear's *mal de mer* – though this year it was air-sickness – would, as usual, simply have to run its course. There was also the psychiatrist and his beautiful young wife, though she hadn't spoken two words to them, merely nodded cordially across her table at luncheon yesterday. Of course, they were in love and perhaps still too physical to be in any way probable. But it was worth a try. She had never known a psychiatrist.

There was also, though she had not even seen him, Eduard Poussard, the mysterious gentleman who occupied the 'penthouse' terrace – the artist who had demanded a north light and who had on arrival ordered a bottle of *obala* sent to his room. There had not been a drop in the hotel and they had immediately to dispatch a *buedera* to fetch a supply from the village. The *buedera* was lame, half the day was gone before she returned, and the artist in the meantime had four times called on the phone, demanding the manager and speaking to everyone in a most unpleasant and irate manner.

Mrs Carter's eyes returned to the actress.

'Tell me about your work,' she said. 'Do you make a great deal of money?'

'Not a great deal,' the young woman replied, 'but enough. I have made only two pictures. This winter I am going to Hollywood. *They* have called me. There I shall make millions. And work – is work. It is something to do.'

'I am the wealthiest woman in the world,' Mrs Carter confided wearily, as if wealth were quite distasteful. 'At least it seems so at times. I receive many statements daily telling how much money I have made. But I was never one for figures. I simply sign the statements, as I must, and return them to my agents.'

She paused, thinking a moment. 'It must be satisfying to work. I have always wondered about people who do – and been just a bit envious. Oh, I have tried – many times. I have visited children in hospitals, and old soldiers in old soldiers' homes. Once' – she smiled shyly – 'I was Recreation Adviser to the Chief Minister of the Government of Singapore at the invitation of the Asia Foundation. – And another time' – she laughed – 'I walked through Grand Central Station – that is in New York City, you know – jingling a little cardboard container for cerebral palsy. I ended up by filling it myself.'

She shook her head sadly, sighing. 'No – when you are very wealthy, you cannot work. You simply try to think of new ways to give your money away. And I have thought of them all. I even' – she smiled somewhat sheepishly – 'spent a season in Africa. It was in my mind to build a hospital, you know – though it wasn't exactly an *original* idea, was it? – import the best of doctors and treat all those rare tropical diseases. I was forever seeing photos of little native children with swollen bellies or various fungus growths on their backs. They broke my heart.'

'What happened?' the actress inquired.

'Well, I don't know,' Mrs Carter replied. 'Many things. There was a typhoon – or whatever those terrible storms are they always have in Africa. The hospital was no more than half built when everything was levelled to the ground – every stick, every stone.'

She had removed her sunglasses to stare broodingly at the sea. Now she turned back to the actress, her eyes vacant, her expression fleetingly pained.

'I felt dreadful,' she murmured. '*Never* have I felt so depressed. But would you believe it?' – she laughed, as quickly happy as she had been sad – 'I was *still* determined. I am not easily discouraged, you know. And I vowed, I *vowed* I would have a hospital, no matter what.'

She leaned forward now, to tilt her huge lace-fringed umbrella against the sun.

'I would have, too,' she concluded, settling back in the shade, 'except that – well, the next night, the very night after I'd vowed, I was bitten by a tiny insect with a long Latin name.' She threw her hands forward in a hopeless gesture. 'The following day I was delirious, and for two weeks after that. I lost sixty-two pounds.

'Not,' she added, brightening, 'not that losing weight is bad, but truly, I was a living skeleton and had to be flown to Cairo on a stretcher and then to Paris after they had injected me with serums or whatever it is they do when you have been bitten by one of those awful insects. My recovery took all of nine months.' She paused. 'My third husband – he was my second George – was alive then, and he advised me that I must *not* start a hospital in Africa. You see, as ill as I was, I was *still* determined, and was secretly planning a second safari. But he found some of my notes under my pillow. I had a most untrustworthy nurse – really a vicious, sneaky woman. Carrie Jones – I remember that name. Wouldn't you know with a name like that! In any event, she spied on me – and told George about the notes under my pillow.'

Mrs Carter sighed deeply. 'I was inconsolable, of course, until George promised – when I was well – to take me to Haiti.' She shook her head, compressing her lips briefly. 'But he died a month later.'

'I'm sorry,' the actress murmured.

'Thank you, my dear.'

Mrs Carter's eyes were downcast; she brooded again, one hand toying with the sand.

3

'I NEVER did get to Haiti,' Mrs Carter said sadly. 'That is one place I have never been. I don't know *why* – perhaps because of George, perhaps because we had planned it together. I have thought about it since – many times – and one day I'd like to go.'

The thought dispelled her sadness. She smiled at the actress, her blue eyes crinkling in anticipated pleasure. 'I am anxious to study voodoo, you know, and observe all those strange primitive rites. I was taken to Fiji when I was a girl, but that isn't nearly as interesting as Haiti, is it? – though I did witness a firewalk. And let me tell you it is true what you have heard about it, every word. They heat a pit of stones until it is white hot; then they go down by the river for their incantations and other things. When they come back their faces are like dolls', with the eyes turned in their heads. Then, as calmly as you please, they walk over the stones in their bare feet without as much as raising a blister – some of them with babies in their arms! – I will admit that one or two of them *ran* – but I noticed that *they* were the younger ones who probably had not learned their incantations quite as well as the others.'

She paused to offer the actress a cigarette, an Egyptian brand of great rarity, and after lighting it and her own, she added: 'Of course, after you've done it – walked on fire, that is – anyone can shrug and say "So what?" That's what my father said at the time. But he was always so *pessimistic* about such things. When we saw the whirling dervishes, the only comment he made was that they gave him a headache. I'm sure Mildred could never stand them with her inner ear – the whirling dervishes, I mean. She would be dizzy in an instant. That is why I have advised her never to see them. But I have never had ear trouble of any kind whatsoever. I have been most fortunate in that respect. . . .'

She smiled at the actress. 'So you see, I *have* tried to work. And when I failed so miserably each time, I thought finally that I would make a career of my home. I didn't *have* a home, of course, but I decided I *would* have one – and give up this eternal travelling. It does grate on one's nerves after a while. I thought I might even have a child, and though I was tired of marriage, I was determined to try it once more – just to see, you know. Well' – she made a sour face, 'it was no better than the others. I found out I *couldn't* have a child, and Henry – he was my fourth husband – didn't want one anyway. Whenever he talked about them – children, that is – you could just *see* the picture he had in his mind: fevered little bodies always smelling vaguely of urine – forever clinging to you with grubby hands, demanding lollypops and ice cream.'

'Ah – I know *exactly* what he meant,' the actress said with a laugh, remembering her brothers and sisters in Rome. 'Your Henry and I would have gotten along.'

' – But I don't see children that way at *all*,' Mrs Carter returned. 'In fact, I was hoping to adopt one, no matter what Henry said. I didn't of course, but if people tell you children are difficult to adopt, never believe them. They are in America, I am told – all sorts of credentials are required. But it is foolish to insist on having an *American* child, don't you think? Americans are so odd. Just because they *are* American, nothing will do but that they have an American child. It has no advantages I can see. In Arabia

14

you can pick children off the streets. In fact, it is difficult to pass through the country without acquiring at least *one* child. I remember the difficult time I had in Riyadhjiji. That's on the very edge of the Mosuljask desert, you know, and very wild. The natives are nomads. I'm sure they must fornicate in the wilderness for a whole year, and then, the following year – usually in the wintertime when they can appear more pathetic – bring all their babies to Riyadhjiji to palm them off on the tourists.'

She laughed. 'I am exaggerating, of course, but truly, that is the impression one gets. Why I remember – I had great trouble with one young mother. I had done her a small favour – I've even forgotten what – and in return she wanted to give me one of her babies! I was astonished! – and refused of course, but I couldn't get her to understand. I don't think she spoke more than two words of English and I knew nothing of her language at all. If I lived a thousand years I could never understand their alphabet. All the characters are like tiny pitchforks lying upside down. In any event, through gestures and by pointing to a picture in a magazine I told her that back home where I came from, across the sea, I had *twenty-four* babies of my own. I don't know *why* I thought of twenty-four, except that, clearly, four or five would have made no impression on her whatsoever. She had twelve of her own, and I probably thought I might as well double it. And let me tell you it *did* work. You should have seen her face! . . . so full of pity and sympathy. Why the very next day . . .'

Mrs Carter stopped abruptly, her face somewhat stricken. ' – I seem to be talking a great deal this morning. And I'm really not that way, you know. If there's anything I can't stand it's a woman who rambles on about everything under the sun – and none of it at all interesting most

15

of the time. Why the others are always saying to me, "Marion, why are you so quiet?" – or "Marion, you haven't said a word in two hours." But I can't help it, really. I believe it's constitutional or organic – something to do with my genes or my glands. There are born talkers – and then there are people like myself – the *thinkers* and *brooders*. I don't mean in the intellectual sense – goodness, no! – but the *wonderers* – the people who would much rather listen than talk. I'm talking now only because we're new to each other and there's so much "catching up" to do before the others arrive. Once they do, I won't get a word in edgewise. They are great talkers, all of them. Except Mildred, perhaps. – But I take that back. She did talk last summer; it was her second summer and I suppose she had grown less timid about expressing herself before the others. The Countess is enough to frighten anyone. I don't mean *physically* – she is a beautiful woman, really astonishing – but the way she talks – and *talks*. Her name is Victoria – Victoria Vranogrec-Markovici. And Robert, of course, is a writer – and you know how *they* like to talk. His full name is Robert R. M. Hunter. Perhaps you've heard the name or read one of his books——'

The actress shook her head. She sat up now, cross-legged like a yogi, and reached for her bottle of suntan lotion.

'I don't know what the R.M. stands for,' Mrs Carter continued, 'but he teaches at a university and writes books, and more books – and articles for various *literary* journals. His luggage consists mainly of typewriters. He brought *three* with him last year. I remember – one was an electric machine, which immediately blew out a fuse. We have DC current, you know, so if you have any electrical appliances with you . . .'

'Is he married?' the actress inquired.

'No; he's not. Nor was he ever. – Can you do that yourself? – here, let me——' and Mrs Carter began smoothing the lotion across the young woman's shoulders and back. ' – Like yourself, he is busy. He lived with his mother most of his adult life, though he is not old, understand; he must be forty-something; it's so hard to tell with a man – but she died several years ago. I met her once. Quite an impressive woman I must say, though the time I spent with her seemed more like an interview for a position than a tea-time chat. I do believe she was afraid I was a candidate for Robert's affections! – she had no idea how old I was, nor the *kind* of relationship I had with her son. But about Robert. I remember – last summer he was doing an article for the *Partisan Review*. That is an American magazine, you know, though I am told it is very well liked at the universities, and quite dignified. I read the manuscript. It was all about "writing" – about "the novel" in particular, which he maintained is a *genre* that has exhausted itself and is *moribund*. That was the word he used – *moribund*. Do you know what it means?'

'I do not,' the actress replied. 'I have never heard such a word.'

'Well, I hadn't either. I had to look it up. It means *dying* . . . simply that. These writers, you know! – they will use *any* word rather than call a thing by its name. – In any event, he compared the novel to epic poetry. "*Who*," he asked, and it was in italics, "*Who reads epic poetry today?*" Of course I had no ready answer, though I thought about it, nor would I dare criticise Robert in any way; he is much too clever and mature and knows everything that is worth knowing, but I must confess that I thought him *wrong* about the novel. How can it be a *genre* that has exhausted itself? Why almost the very first sentence a child learns to speak is "Tell me a story". They are constantly saying that, and if anyone is exhausted

17

it must be their parents who are having to think up all these stories to tell them. And that is why *I* maintain – though I wouldn't dare tell Robert – that we shall *always* have novelists. They are simply our parents and we are still children saying "Tell me a story". Though I do confess that some of the stories *they* tell are a little strange. I have never favoured pornography in literature – it seems such an *easy* way to get someone's attention – but where can you find a book nowadays that doesn't have something like that in it, unless it's a cookery book – and even those are not above suspicion. I knew a woman once who read nothing but cookery books until her analyst told her that it was *oral* gratification, and that half a cup of this and a teaspoonful of that were merely *symbols* for something *not* so innocent, I can assure you. . . .'

4

'If you lie on your stomach that way,' Mrs Carter said to the actress, 'I would advise putting the lotion on the soles of your feet – just in case, you know. By ten o'clock the sun of Corbodéra will be intense. It will press down upon you like a great weight.'

'I have a good skin for the sun,' the actress replied; 'I never burn badly.'

'I can see that,' Mrs Carter observed. 'It has an olive tinge, a touch of gold. If you don't mind my saying so, you are a very beautiful young woman.'

'Yes, I know,' the actress agreed. 'I am lucky. If I had no beauty, I would have nothing.'

'Nonsense! You would have your talent.'

The actress shrugged.

'My body is my talent. Oh – my voice, too, I am told. It is husky. And now I know how to use it.'

'But you are an actress!'

'Three years ago I was not an actress. I was nothing. – A waitress, a cook. I made pizzas in a restaurant window for all to see. – Until I found out they were not looking at the pizzas.'

Mrs Carter smiled and then laughed heartily. 'You *are* funny. – Humorous, I mean. And next you will tell me that *he* was not looking at the pizzas either.'

'*He?*'

'Yes. – Come now. *Someone* discovered you. Someone came to the window – some well-known Italian producer or director – and there you were, making pizzas.'

The actress was astonished. 'But how did you know!'

'It was easy,' Mrs Carter replied, reaching forward to pat the young woman's hand. '*You* told me. What else could possibly have happened? You could have been in the deepest coal mine in Wales, with the black all over your face, and they would have come down with lights on their heads to find you. There is no place you could possibly hide! Your destiny is written all over you. And in America, believe me, you will be a fantastic success. Tell me – who was he?'

'Roberto Razizi.'

Mrs Carter raised her eyebrows. 'I have heard of him. Indeed, I have heard that name. You will forgive me if I do not see many films. Somehow I am never in a country where there are any. Or if there are, they are American – one of those terrifying musicals or westerns. – I am told that Roberto Razizi is a real artist. And he . . . *made* you, so to speak?'

'Not "so to speak". He made me. Day and night. I spent two of the hardest years of my life being "made". It was not much different from that play – what is it? – *Pygmalion*? "Italian is a soft language," he would say; "it is to be whispered and hummed – not tossed around and hammered to death like a pizza." Always the pizza. He never let me forget. It was always – "What can I expect from a pizza-maker?" – I learned English too, of course. You must speak English or you are dead. And,' she added as an afterthought, 'he was my lover. It was part of our bargain. To him it meant a lot; to me, nothing. With Roberto, it was like brushing my teeth or running up the shade in the morning. But do not misunderstand. He is a great man. A great artist. When he said "cry" to me, I became a river. When he asked me to be angry, I was ready to kill. When he said I was gentle, loving – ah, I melted: I became a Madonna. He has a great gift. No one has such a gift. But as a lover – no; I could have slept with a pizza with more pleasure. He gave all to his work. I have seen him cry like a baby and kick at furniture when a scene was not going well – but to his women he gave nothing – only what was left – a shell, a tired boy's body that was fifty years old. Yes – you would be amazed – a boy's body, and what it wanted most of all was to be held and comforted, rocked in my arms.' She shrugged. 'So that is what I did. I held him. I rocked. And we went on making the pictures.'

'But that is *fascinating*,' Mrs Carter cried. '*People* are fascinating. I don't know of *anything* more fascinating.'

'They are coming now,' the actress said, glancing over her shoulder. '– The American and his wife. They are going swimming.'

'Heavens!' Mrs Carter exclaimed. She turned to look. '– I have forgotten your name. Or perhaps I never asked.'

'Gia Imola.'

'Of *course*. I have seen that name. Or heard it. I will introduce you if they stop by. – She *is* very pretty. And a modest bathing suit, I must say. I am tired of all this nakedness. Last summer we were drowned in flesh. The object seems to be to show every square inch short of indecent exposure. There was even a nudist colony a little way up the beach – on the Government property. They surrounded it with wire, but I had connections, and as a lark most of us spent a day there. It was unpleasant really. Everyone spoke in hushed tones – as if there were something *holy* in the vicinity, or as if someone had died. And everyone is always looking straight ahead, or *up*. I had a stiff neck by the time I left, though I must admit I did look *down* once in a while, and felt very guilty and impure for doing so. But what is the point if you must

21

always look up? It is much easier to wear clothes, and far less draughty.'

The American and his wife were quite close now.

'They *do* see us,' Mrs Carter whispered. 'They *are* going to stop.' She raised her voice cheerily – 'Hello there!'– and smiled and waved.

'This is Gia Imola,' she said, 'the famous film star. And I am Mrs Carter, Mrs Wainwright Carter, the third, though in recent years I have grown used to calling myself Mrs Marion Carter. That is the way I sign all my cheques.'

'I am Paul Dier,' the young man replied, smiling broadly, 'which is the way I sign all my cheques. And this is Suzette Dier. She is not a movie actress. She is my wife.'

Now that was a pleasant and unusual thing to say! But they were obviously alive in their love; it must have been transforming the world. Corbodéra, ordinarily beautiful, must have seemed breath-taking to them – the sea a jewel, the sky so blue it hurt, and the hotel, an architectural monstrosity at best, must have been described on the postcards – if they found time to write at all – as 'quaint, picturesque, so "old-fashioned" and charming it would warm your heart'. Had they met Count Dracula on the beach this morning they probably would have thrown their arms about him and kissed his blood-flecked cheek.

Both were young and good-looking, slender, strong, with clear eyes and skin and a good coat of tan already. The wife was not beautiful as she had seemed to Mrs Carter at a distance – or perhaps it was simply that she suffered in comparison with the actress with whom she stood talking and with whom no one, unless it was the Countess ten years younger, could possibly compare. She was certainly pleasant to look at, however, with a knotted sweep of thick honey-coloured hair that brought Gia's eyes back for a second close look.

'I must explain about the sea,' Mrs Carter said promptly; 'do sit down, both of you; just for a moment. The tide is coming in, so it will be better to swim later anyway.'

She made a space for them on the sand between the actress and herself, moving the fly corpses back to surround the four of them.

5

'You are lucky to be here now,' Mrs Carter said to the Diers, 'because later, in August, the sea becomes phosphorescent and slightly oily to the touch. It puzzled me for years, but last year a visiting ichthyologist explained to me that there is a species of crab, a minute creature, understand, that lays its eggs among the rocks.'

She paused long enough for a mysterious, penetrating glance at the sea, then came back with a wide gesture, adding: 'The waters around Corbodéra are alkaline, you know; there is calcimine or calcium – some sort of *chalky* chemistry going on between the stones. In winter I believe the cliffs recede by three inches or more, and I am told that even in summer various deposits drop off into the sea. Indeed, this man, whose credentials I might add were impeccable – I would hesitate to describe the complexity of the apparatus he brought with him as well as the reams of mathematical data – this man claimed that the whole island, *all* of it, understand, will disappear entirely in a matter of some thousands of years. It will . . . *go*; simply vanish, drop down into the sea like Atlantis or Mu.'

'Well, I am certainly glad we are here now,' Paul Dier said, his expression one of vague shock.

'But he also told me,' Mrs Carter continued, ' – and it has some connection with these crabs – they create bubbles, "gaseous pockets" he called them, when they lay their eggs in the chalk – that in another thousand years or so, the island will rise again, come up *out* of the sea.

24

– And so on, the cycle repeating itself. He showed me fossils that prove Corbodéra has disappeared *three* times and risen again. There are fossils everywhere. Why I can hardly take a walk now without coming across some fossil or other. I started collecting them at first, but soon there were so many in my room that the maid complained about dusting them. Isn't that interesting?'

Suzette Dier parted her lips as if to answer Mrs Carter but then made no sound. She seemed momentarily disorientated – staring at the sea of Corbodéra as if in the next moment a tidal wave might rise and sweep the island from beneath her feet. She then turned, glancing back at the towering white chalk cliffs that surrounded the hotel on three sides. Her husband, however, was smiling broadly at Mrs Carter, and he now said exactly what the actress had said moments ago: 'I have never heard of anything *more* interesting. And I have heard a great many interesting things in my life.'

'That is because you are a psychiatrist,' Mrs Carter returned. 'They hear *all* the interesting things.' She instantly covered her mouth. 'I should not have said that! – But you might as well know: I *own* the Polonaise, as well as most of the island – not Tanique: the Government of Spain wished to retain its fishing interests – though as I was telling Miss Imola, I prefer to keep it a secret – about the Polonaise, I mean. If there is anything I detest it is preferential treatment. Only my hotel agent knows, and it is he who keeps out the undesirables. I should not want Corbodéra to become like Majorca, simply teeming with tourists. They are now *organised*, I am told, and have *social* directors who arrange tours and badminton. One hotel has an orchestra. It is Spanish, fortunately, but you can be sure it will be only a matter of time before they import an *American* orchestra. Next they will organise a baseball team. And that, of course, will be the end. It will be worse than the Continent. There is not a spot, not a square inch where you can even breathe on the Continent. Surely you have noticed.'

Suzette Dier had apparently regained her composure, and with it her voice. 'In a way we must have,' she replied, linking her arm with her husband's. 'That is why we are here. We wanted a quiet, secluded place.' Her smile was disarming as she added: 'But tell us more, Mrs Carter. – About the island, I mean. And the ichthyologist. My mind is filled with images. I think of the *Sunken Cathedral.*'

'Why yes,' Mrs Carter returned promptly, very pleased. 'It does give rise to all sorts of speculations, doesn't it? – if one has an active mind, which I am told I have. I like to imagine, for example, that the Polonaise will remain intact, survive the deluge so to speak. It is very strong, you know. Have you noticed the walls? – they are solid stone and three feet thick. Not a nail was used in the entire structure. Everything simply *rests* on top of each other, held up – or down – by gravity. I believe it served as a fortification in ancient times, before the Mongols or the Normans – whoever those barbarians were – swept down from the west and ravaged Rome. Of course' – she turned to look back at the hotel – 'the roof will go; it is very flimsy, but that will add to its charm. My only regret, unlike *you*, Doctor Dier, is that I am here now, *before* the island goes, and not afterwards to see it rise. It almost tempts one to become a Buddhist. – Not transmigration, of course; no, I would need all my *human* faculties to see Corbodéra rise – but reincarnation. The trouble *there*, however, is memory. I would not remember Corbodéra; I would think I had never seen it before. I do confess I have found something wrong with every religion.

One is always so optimistic at first. Every time I become interested in a new one, I think – *Ah*, this is it. But after you've gone a little way, there is always *something* unpleasant and not at all what you'd like. Somehow you become "lost" – and it is a most uncomfortable feeling. The Catholics are very good in that respect – at least you know exactly *where* you are, and that there are only two, or perhaps three, places to go. – Though I will confess that spiritualism has the most appeal for me. There was a medium two summers ago whom we all went to visit at Turegano. That is quite close to Madrid if you do not know it. Of course there were the bulls – everyone was going to see the bulls, but I noticed they all turned up at Señora Calazada's beforehand. She broke eggs into a bowl and stirred with some sort of little stick – they all have a different method you know – and then went into a trance. She rambled on in a few foreign languages but then settled on English. I was glad of that; I do so hate to have the spirits translated. But her control was a child, a little girl. It was an *Indian* guide, an *American* Indian, and I am so tired of those; they seem to populate the whole of the spirit world. I often wonder how they manage to "get through" so easily. In any event, this one was called "Sleepy Waters", and I must say I was disappointed. But I listened, and the child was sweet enough. She told all about her tribe; they were the "river people", whatever that is, and made pottery which they painted. She introduced us to her mother, who was very nice, too, I must say, though she didn't speak English as well, and then she brought one of my husbands – my first George – to speak to me. He hadn't changed a bit – and was even irritated that he had been called at all. Evidently he had been doing something important, though he didn't say what. I had the silly idea he might have been in the bathroom – if they do have bathrooms, and I believe they must. It isn't so different from here, you know. You'd be astonished at the sameness. Why, Sir Oliver Lodge reported *cigars*! In any event, George was quite rude – the way he always was if I had to speak to him through the bathroom door. But sometimes it was necessary. The phone was forever ringing – and it was always for George. I got very few calls in those days. . . .'

The others were listening so avidly that Mrs Carter had the impression they wanted her to go on forever. But there was a slight ache in her throat and she had forgotten to bring her lozenges with her

'We will have lunch together,' she promised, smiling at the actress and then at the honeymooners.' – The four of us. I want to hear more; it's all too fascinating about the film industry and about being a psychiatrist. I would invite Mildred Hawkins to join us – she arrived yesterday, you know – but the poor soul was air-sick all the way and won't be herself for a day or two.' She added, with a penetrating look at Paul Dier: 'I do wonder if *that* couldn't be psychogenic . . . all this nonsense about the labyrinth of her inner ear. It may be all in her mind. Perhaps one day when you are not too busy you will have a look at her. She's a schoolteacher. you know. From Pennsylvania.' She turned to the actress. 'Pennsylvania is a state in *America*. I have always liked that name. It has a poetic ring. And I do believe Sleepy Waters came from there. Yes, I'm sure she did. I remember asking Señora Calazada. . . .'

6

ROBERT R. M. HUNTER was the next to arrive, his temper short, his nerves ragged because his journey had been plagued by a series of small accidents. For one thing, his attaché case, filled with notes for a projected work, had slipped through his fingers as his ship docked and disappeared into the dark and muddy waters of coastal Spain. Later, as he waited at customs, a woman, a stranger whom he had jostled in the crowd, had, like a sudden maniac, begun beating him over the head with her umbrella while he stood defenceless and amazed. The police had to push their way through tens of curious spectators before the foolish woman was convinced that he had not 'attacked' her at all, but had been merely pushed against her by the crowd.

He greeted Mrs Carter with deliberate, thinking warmth, was barely cordial to the Diers, and stared at the actress with such disbelief that her name had to be repeated three times before he heard it. He then disappeared into his suite for a warm bath, a tray of food, and a 'nap' that lasted the better part of three days.

When he appeared he was quite himself again, and just in time to greet the Countess who arrived by chartered helicopter and was deposited on the lawn of the Polonaise.

'Wouldn't you know!' Mrs Carter exclaimed as she watched Victoria step from the plane. She felt herself blushing and her glance at the Diers was full of apology.

'But she is really not affected,' she explained. 'This is not a silly act to impress us; if there were no one on the island at all she would have come that way if it pleased her. There must be *some* logical reason.'

And there was. Its name was Nicholas Passanante, and it stepped from the plane behind the Countess. It was a boy, surely no older than fourteen, who all too soon revealed that he had not a virtue to recommend him except a face that was more angel than child.

'Nicky had never been up in a plane,' the Countess said in brief explanation. She greeted the others warmly, nodded at the Diers, and immediately inquired after the *geistata*.

'The "swarming" was over yesterday,' Mrs Carter reassured her. 'I asked the Constable; he has charts and things, you know, and he is quite sure. They are gone earlier this year. I believe it had something to do with the vernal equinox. So you are quite safe.'

The Countess looked relieved.

'This is Nicky,' she said, brushing a lock of hair from the child's forehead. '– Nicholas Passanante.' The boy shuffled from one foot to the other and swallowed audibly as he murmured a few shy words of greeting. The Countess added: 'Be kind to him; he has had a dreadful time.' She touched Nicky's chin, turning his face to hers. 'Are you hungry? Come. I will show you the kitchen and the cook.' And with that they disappeared.

'It's his face!' Mrs Carter said promptly. 'Surely he has a profile that would make your heart stop.'

'Passanante,' murmured Mildred Hawkins who, palely, was reclining in a deck chair sipping lemon juice and water. She was still not entirely well. She had come down for a few moments of sunshine and fresh air and had stayed when the Countess's plane began hovering over the hotel.

'Passanante,' she repeated with an inquiring look at the

30

others. The name was Italian but the boy's accent had seemed distinctly American.

Robert was something of an authority on languages and accents. 'He's from Brooklyn,' he said without hesitation.

Mrs Carter was amazed.

'Brooklyn!' she repeated. She turned to the actress. 'That is a place in New York – a sort of city *jungle*. Why I remember . . .'

She was instantly silent because the artist had appeared. He was good-looking and well-built, trimly bearded, and wore nothing but his sandals and something that looked like a tangled fishnet for bathing trunks, a towel slung across his shoulder. He nodded vaguely in the direction of everyone as he made his way across the pavilion to the beach.

'Who is *that*?' Mildred inquired, sitting up.

'Poussard,' Mrs Carter replied. 'The artist. I *told* you. He has spoken to no one at all.'

'We have talked,' Suzette Dier said. 'Paul and I had a drink with him.'

'He is Eduard Poussard,' Paul Dier said. 'He has a brother Henri. They both paint. Their work is fairly well known.'

'I have never heard of him,' Mildred murmured, reclining once more. 'Or his brother either. His bathing suit is disgusting.'

Nicky had come back, his mouth stuffed. He sat himself on the balustrade, his legs swinging, munching a huge bologna sandwich. Everyone stared at him in silence.

'Where is Victoria?' Mrs Carter asked gently. The boy's face was so beautiful it awed her, despite the stuffed cheeks, the chomping jaws.

Either the child was hard of hearing or didn't understand. Mrs Carter repeated the question, and a third time.

31

'Oh – *Vicky*,' he said suddenly, his face brightening. 'She's in the kitchen talking to the cook.'

'How long have you been with her?' Mrs Carter pried, unable to take her eyes off him.

'With who?'

'The Countess. – Victoria. – Very well, with *Vicky*.'

'Oh – I don't know. A couple of months.'

'But what do you and Victoria *do*? I mean——' She was embarrassed and turned to the others with a laugh. 'Mildred, *you* talk to him,' she whispered. 'You're used to children.'

But the boy had jumped from his perch and was making his way across the sand toward the water. A few moments later, the Countess returned carrying a large bowl of soup which she was eating as if she were starved. She sat on the balustrade and interrupted her soup long enough to stare with pleasure through the forest of *pedrosa* trees and the banks of *cazalla* blazing against the hotel walls. 'It is good to be back,' she sighed. 'Corbodéra is beautiful this year. More beautiful than I have ever seen it.'

Mrs Carter, who was something of a horticulturist, reminded her of the seven-year *valdepeñas*. 'It will bloom this year,' she said. 'There is only one bud but it is the size of your fist.' She explained to the Diers: 'We have been waiting five years to see the *valdepeñas* flower. No one knows what it looks like, not even Señor Gutiérrez – he's our Constable. – It is the most amazing plant. Do go to see it some evening when you walk. It is beyond Señor Gutiérrez's office on the way to the village. It is growing in the ruins of a church.' She turned back to the Countess who was suddenly apprehensive.

'Where is Nicky?' she demanded, glancing about quickly.

'*There*,' Mrs Carter said, 'by the shore. He is taking off

his shoes to wade. – See how far the artist has gone! Clearly, he is a powerful swimmer.'

The Countess raised her voice.

'Be careful, Nicky! Do not cut your feet!' She turned back to the others with a sigh. 'Ah Nicky. So sad. Always so sad. I live only to see him smile. Never have I seen him smile, not in the two months he has been with me.' She kept her eyes on the boy who had rolled the legs of his slim trousers to the knees and was now ankle-deep in the water. '– I have given him everything I could think of. He does not like toys. Clothes mean nothing to him. His eyes were bright on the plane. *That* interested him; but we cannot spend all of our time in the air, can we? And even that did not make him happy.' She added sadly, almost in a whisper, 'What is happiness?'

'Our Dr Dier is a *psychiatrist*,' Mrs Carter told her in an intimate and revelatory manner.

'– Ah, is that so?' Victoria faced Paul, fastening her great dark eyes on him in a melancholy stare. 'And psychiatrists are merchants of the soul. They see *all* the unhappy people and make them happy.'

There was a pause. Everyone made 'room', so to speak, for Paul to tell them the secret of happiness. He shifted uncomfortably in his chair, glancing at his wife.

'I don't know why it is,' he began, 'but the word "psychiatrist" has a magic ring to it. We're mortal – and quite ordinary people. We have no secrets, no special knowledge that isn't available to anyone who will trouble himself to find it.'

'You're not getting off that easily,' Robert said with a teasing smile. 'Come now – *happiness*.'

Paul shrugged. 'Basically – I would say that it consists of getting, and giving, those things which made us happy as a child.'

33

'How true,' Mrs Carter sighed. 'We are all so very passionate when we're young. To desire something then is to desire the whole of life; it crowds everything out of existence. Why I remember——'

But before she could remember in detail, Mildred Hawkins spoke, disagreeing with the psychiatrist.

'I teach grade school,' she said. 'I have children with me constantly, and they seem to want *silly* things. I have taken them to the beach and seen them fight over a square foot of sand when the sand stretched for miles around them.'

'They weren't fighting over the sand,' Paul smiled. 'They were fighting to see whom you loved the most – and to whom you would give that precious foot of sand.'

'I thought they all wanted to sleep with their mothers,' Robert said.

'They do,' Paul replied. 'But most of them are finally content to sleep with their wives.'

'And some of them with themselves,' the Countess announced sonorously, between mouthfuls of soup. 'I had one husband who wouldn't allow me to get into bed with him for three months after we were married. Once I came upon him when he was nude and he behaved like a school-boy – pulling his knees together and covering his private parts with his hands. "What is this!" I asked, "– have you the crown jewels of Russia hidden between your legs?"– If I had such a husband now I would kill him – or cut off his jewels and make a pendant for my throat. But husbands are for the very young. When you are my age and have seen what I have seen, they are like the spun sugar you buy at a circus . . . sticky and sweet and full of hot air. You bite into it and find you have a mouthful of nothing.'

Robert's eyes were still on the psychiatrist.

'I am not satisfied,' he said.

Paul smiled and shrugged. 'Well, then, let me see. . . . You want a fancier definition, obviously.' He thought for a moment. ' – It is easier to begin by defining *un*happiness. Those whose capacity for love is impaired – they are the unhappy ones; and those who submit to *irrational* authority, who do not create, so to speak, a morality of their own based on knowledge. Happiness is an absence of these anomalies – because they *are* anomalies. I believe happiness on the whole is a *natural* state – and by "happiness" I don't mean "euphoria" or any of those moments of heightened pleasure when one is – well, extraordinarily successful, let us say, or falling in love.'

'But that is to neglect sorrow,' Robert objected, 'pain. . . .'

'Clearly, these give happiness its meaning,' Paul replied. 'Happiness could not be known – would have no existence at all, of course, without sorrow and pain.'

'You are not a psychiatrist,' Robert concluded; 'you are a Zen patriarch.'

Paul gestured indifferently. 'I would be the last to claim that knowledge is the exclusive property of science. But I know very little about Zen.'

'I spent a year in Japan,' Mrs Carter said. 'I knew several of those people.'

'What people?' Mildred inquired. Her voice seemed peevish; probably she was still a bit queasy, and Mrs Carter leaned forward to pat her hand comfortingly.

'Why the Zenists, or the Zenites – whatever they're called. I remember – there was a young Armenian there who insisted I try a koan or two.'

'A what?' Gia asked.

'A koan,' Mrs Carter replied. 'Those are their queer sayings, such as, "What is the sound of one hand clap-

35

ping?" You choose a saying – or are given one I believe –
if you are in a monastery, and then you think about it for
several years. Of course' – she smiled at Suzette Dier who
was listening more carefully than the others – 'I wasn't
prepared to spend several years on a koan; my husband –
that was my first George – would never have permitted it;
but I did want to try – just to see, you know. So I made
up my own koan.'

'Which was——?' Robert inquired.

Mrs Carter hesitated, slightly embarrassed. ' "To be, is
not to be." ' She added in a rush: 'It must be *illogical*, you
know, and I thought a little modified Shakespeare
wouldn't hurt.'

'And did it?' Robert asked. 'What happened?'

'Well it drove me crazy,' Mrs Carter confessed, 'which
is precisely what it's supposed to do, but I was up all hours
of the night. I don't know how often George woke up
and saw me sitting in a chair staring into space. "What in
heaven's name are you doing?" he would ask. "I am saying my koan," I'd reply.' She broke into a laugh. '*Fortunately* – we left Japan the following week – else I would *still*
be saying my koan.'

The Countess was not listening. She was staring toward
the sea.

'Nicky,' she called, 'be careful. You are too deep.'

'He's barely up to his knees,' Gia Imola reassured her.

' – But there are currents; the rocks are mossy.'

'He's a very good-looking boy,' Suzette Dier said. 'It is
hard to keep one's eyes off him.'

'I never do,' the Countess replied. 'That is his work. To
be seen. That is his talent. God gave him a great gift.'

'I spoke to him in Italian,' Gia said, 'but he did not
understand.'

'Nicky? He is not Italian. His grandfather was. He is

36

American. He is as American as the hot dog, and shall turn into one if he does not stop eating them. Thank God there are no hot dogs on Corbodéra.' She looked at Mrs Carter severely. 'And if you have any of that awful American "coke" in your cellars, I shall leave tomorrow. He drank gallons in Rome – until his skin broke out. I had to fill him with so many vitamins he was peeing green.'

'But where did you find him?' Mrs Carter inquired. 'We have been dying of curiosity.'

'Ah – it is too sad,' the Countess replied. 'But one day I will tell you. Tomorrow – or next week; after I have rested and found my strength.'

'You were in America this winter!' Mrs Carter accused.

'No. No, I spent the whole of the year in Rome. I was having my portrait painted.' She turned to the others. 'I have been to America only once, one winter three years ago, after I lost André.'

She might have been talking about a husband, or a lover, or even a child, but Paul Dier, watching her, had the curious impression she was talking about a pet. However, she did not say. Only – 'I wanted to forget. Conchita was with me then; she hired a limousine. – And we toured!' She gestured as if 'touring' were an extraordinary thing to do. ' – Back and forth, east and west. It is a very large country, you know; I thought it would never end; and varied – I must say that for it. When you get very far west, the landscape is astonishing; I thought I was on the moon. Conchita was so frightened, I had to calm her several times. "It is *only* America," I said to her. "There is no need to stare out the window so. If you cannot bear it, then shut your eyes or read your book." But she remained quite nervous. She could not wait until we got to a *motel* in the evening. Then she would lock all the doors

37

and pull down the shades – to keep out the landscape, you know.'

'Did you see Los Angeles?' Mrs Carter inquired.

'Why yes,' the Countess replied. ' – A beautiful name.'

'I have a sister there,' Mrs Carter mused. 'If I had known you were going at the time, I would have posted a letter and you could have visited. She is a marvellous cook, always fussing in the kitchen. – Even as a little girl. I remember – she had a toy stove, but it burned real wood – and coal! – If you could find pieces small enough to fit. And every rainy afternoon she would bake tiny cakes which she frosted with coloured icing. They were *delicious*. – I blame her now for the fact that I am overweight. I believe I eat everything in sight simply because I am hoping to find somewhere, in some part of the world, one of her dear little cakes.' She glanced quickly at Paul Dier for possible confirmation, but the psychiatrist's face remained impassive.

'Did you spend any time in New York?' Mildred Hawkins inquired of the Countess. 'New York *is* America. It epitomises its culture.'

'Why yes,' Victoria replied. 'We were there for several weeks. I saw everything – the ballet, the opera, the museums – many plays, and all the restaurants. It was stimulating. I think I would have enjoyed it if it hadn't been for André. I saw him everywhere. I could not look into a bowl of soup but that his queer little face wasn't staring back at me. – With those eyes – those sad, sad eyes. You remember those eyes?'

Mildred, Robert and Mrs Carter nodded, and the Countess sighed.

'*Sibirsk ust zaisandinsk pskovriev mip undzhachansk,*' she concluded, adding generously for those who did not understand her language: 'Grief travels far.'

Part Two

I

'It is madness,' Eduard Poussard said, growing excited, 'to compare Picasso to Le Fauconnier and de la Fresnave. Duchamp was an infant, Léger a painter of plumbing. I cannot even speak of Gleizes or Metzinger. Braque I can certainly mention if I try. Tanguy was a painter of fæces. He refined and polished them like gems. I cannot imagine why you even think of his name. I forgot it the moment I saw one of his paintings. To mention it – in the same breath with *Picasso*! . . .'

'Picasso, Picasso!' Mildred sang out harshly, making no effort at all to keep the sneer from her face.

'I agree with the artist,' the Countess said. 'Picasso is a great painter, but careless. I cannot forgive carelessness. Never do I forgive carelessness in art. I have wept before some of his paintings: the portraits of boys and of his sweet children . . . little Paul in a clown suit; but others I could spit upon.'

The artist was now so angry, the colour spread from his throat across his chest.

'If Picasso dipped his brush in dung,' he said, biting at his words, 'and spread it across a brick wall, it would *breathe* with fire of life, it would *glow* with fevered energy. . . .'

Mildred couldn't control her outrage. '*Our* Picasso, who art in heaven,' she chanted whitely, 'hallowed be thy name. . . .'

'I like him,' Gia contributed. 'He has a sense of humour.'

'Humour!' Mildred shouted, now so excited the corners of her mouth were flecked with saliva. 'He is an ape and a buffoon! He is a *swindler!* He has perpetrated the greatest hoax in the history of art. He is shameless and lives like the Spanish pig that he is! I would gladly set fire to every canvas he has defiled. He has been the anti-Christ of art, promulgating his pornographic scrawls until the world stinks of his corruption. Art is dead unless it finds the strength to crucify this monster. It has been drowned in the cesspool he has stirred to a maelstrom with his . . . *phallic* brush!'

'There, there,' Mrs Carter said gently, patting Mildred's hand. The girl's lack of restraint, the violent gestures she used, were obviously embarrassing Suzette Dier and enraging the artist. The veins in his neck were a skein of pulsing cords.

'Picasso,' he hissed, 'is the saint, the *saviour* of art. We should all be dead for the next thousand years but for this giant, this hero of the spirit.' He reached forward, his hands grasping, strangling the air between himself and Mildred. ' – There was a glimmer of light in Delacroix, Poussin, Daumier; it brightened in Pissarro, Degas, Lautrec, but Cézanne was John – the voice crying in the wilderness, bringing his holy water – presaging the birth of the hero, the saviour who was Picasso! It is people like you' – he jabbed a finger toward Mildred in a gesture he would have used had he been holding a knife – 'who would crucify the king! You – all of you' – and in his rage he encompassed the others in a sweeping gesture that was a scythe slashing through a field of wheat – 'you are the Pilates of the world, or worse – the crowd milling at the gate – "Give us Barabbas!" – give us anyone at all as long as we can taste blood!'

With this he stood, and in his impatience to leave them,

stumbled and fell as he turned. In a moment he was up, cursing under his breath, stomping towards the hotel. The others stared after him in a slightly embarrassed silence.

'Well!' Mrs Carter said presently, 'we have certainly touched some sore spots this morning. I confess I am disturbed when things get quite so out of hand.' She looked at Mildred archly. 'I do believe you could have expressed your opinions with a little more restraint.'

'They are not opinions,' Mildred returned hotly; 'they're convictions. I feel strongly about painting.'

'Well, we *all* do, my dear,' Mrs Carter said. 'But to call Picasso the anti-Christ of art! Surely that is going a little far.'

'A mere figure of speech,' Robert suggested. 'And an interesting one. Or do you still believe in the devil, Mildred?'

The girl's anger was slow to die. She was breathing heavily and unravelling yards of her knitting as if the last hour's work had displeased her.

'What do you mean – *still*?' she asked irritably.

'Well, you *are* a Catholic.'

'Mildred is *not* a Catholic,' Mrs Carter interrupted quickly, speaking for the girl who seemed quite ready to turn her wrath on Robert if she did not prevent it. 'She was merely *born* into a Catholic family. That was many years ago. – Not too many,' she added, again patting Mildred's hand. 'But when she was in her teens, she realised how atavistic it was and gave it up instantly, though she has retained, wisely, a poetic appreciation for the Mass. I know all about it, don't I, Mildred, because once' – she turned to face the others – 'we had a long and most agreeable discussion about it without either of us losing our tempers.'

43

'I have heard,' Robert said, 'that it is all simply a sneaky way of tapping the incestuous libido, of rendering it impotent and relatively harmless. . . .'

Mildred had stuffed the knitting into her beach bag and without another word or a moment's further delay, rose and marched toward the hotel.

'Perhaps *you* have an opinion, Paul,' Robert continued, his eyes on the psychiatrist. 'You don't say very much. I suppose your profession *conditions* you to silence. You must sit all day and *listen.*'

Paul frowned slightly and glanced quickly at his wife before returning his eyes to Robert.

'Well, as I *listened* to Miss Hawkins and the artist,' he replied, somewhat coolly, 'I was inclined to feel that they represented extremes. I'm sure Picasso is neither as good nor as bad as either of them makes out. As for myself – I enjoy him. I feel he has contributed immeasurably to the riches of the world and of the spirit. – My, wife owns one of his paintings – a small head – one of the first so-called "double-vision" women.'

'I don't mean Picasso,' Robert said peevishly. 'I mean that ghost in the Vatican, that "past of an illusion".' He was obviously ill-tempered this morning and trying to bait even the psychiatrist.

'What *ails* everyone today?' Mrs Carter interrupted quickly. 'Robert – I do believe *you* are the instigator. You know how Mildred feels about Picasso. And you must have discovered the artist's feelings, and so, in your insidious way, you introduced the subject. Don't tell me it is merely research for one of your books! That would be too heartless. – Victoria, do help me until everyone has quieted down. Tell us something interesting and diverting. Tell us about Nicky.'

' – Ah, Nicky,' the Countess replied. She glanced back

toward the hotel. 'Where is he? I have not seen him for hours. I am getting lonely.'

'He went with the Constable,' Mrs Carter said, ' – to see the bud on the *valdepeñas* and then to inspect the *santanella*. There is a whole nest of them this year.' She shook her head quickly. 'You are really most exasperating, Victoria. You know how I loathe secrets. Why, I divorced one of my husbands for exactly that reason. The most exasperating man! – always locking his desk drawers and putting sealing wax on large manila envelopes. For years I thought he was a spy of some sort until I discovered that he simply liked things closed. Everything had to be covered, sealed. Did you ever hear of such a thing! Why, I couldn't keep a jar of jam open on the breakfast table that he didn't break into a sweat and have to clap on the cover and screw it tight. I could barely manage to get a spoonful of jam for my toast in the morning!' She looked at Paul Dier. 'He was an *oil* man, you know; and I'm sure that must be significant – I mean, having to cap all those geysers all the time. I remember – there was always "a big one" coming through. I don't know why every one was a big one, but it always was. The foreman would usually call me on the phone and say, "Tell Henry 'the big one' is coming through." So I would turn to Henry and tell him that, and whenever I did his eyes would get shiny and he would say quietly, "The big one!" in a very faraway voice. Of course, sometimes it would turn out to be only a dribble, or a gas pocket, and then Henry would become ill. He always became ill when that happened. Truly. He would actually go to bed for a day and nothing would do but that he have chicken soup and Jello. – That was in Texas.' She turned to the actress. 'Texas is a state in America. – But what I started to say' – she looked at the Countess severely – 'is that you have been very unkind to us, Victoria. Now I insist. I want to know about Nicky – I want to hear *all* about him.'

'Ah, Nicky,' the Countess replied. She brooded, her melancholy eyes staring at the sea of Corbodéra as if she were seeing a mirage.

'I found him in Rome,' she murmured, and sighed.

Mrs Carter settled comfortably back in her beach chair as she might in a theatre seat when the lights begin to dim and the curtain is about to rise. Her eyes sparkled a little as she glanced at the Diers and when the actress shifted her position on the sand and seemed about to say something, Mrs Carter promptly shushed her.

'He was living in a hot near the slums,' the Countess continued, 'close to Capannor-Mesagne.'

Rarely did her accent confuse the others, but even Robert who, for some reason kept staring at the actress, didn't know what a 'hot' was.

'A *hot*, a *hot*,' the Countess repeated – as if the others were being quite stupid. ' – The kind children build. – Come now; you take sticks and nails and build a small house – a room – out of doors.'

'A hut!' Robert said.

'Yes, a hot,' the Countess replied. 'I used to build them myself; though in Russia there is very little wood. Every-thing is steel and iron.' She turned to the Diers and the actress. 'But I am not Russian; I merely lived there when I was a little girl.' She did not explain further, and it was doubtful that she could, since her lineage was so confused that no country could rightfully claim her as its own. In addition, it seemed impossible to name any country in the world where she hadn't lived for at least a time.

'About Nicky——' Mrs Carter whispered, as if she were backstage cueing an actress.

' – Ah, Nicky,' the Countess replied, her face saddening.

'Tell us what he was *doing* in Rome,' Mrs Carter prompted. 'After all, he *is* an American.'

The Countess nodded. 'He came to Rome with his mother – to visit his paternal grandmother. His father had died, and after the news of her son's death, the grandmother had written that she herself was ill and in fear of dying, and that her last dear wish was to see her grandson.'

'They were *impoverished*, of course,' Mrs Carter anticipated. 'But the grandmother *sent* them the money.'

'Yes,' the Countess replied; 'yes – and she assured them there would be money for their return.'

'But when they arrived,' Mrs Carter said triumphantly, unable to restrain herself – for she knew stories very well, and all life's little ironies, 'the grandmother was *dead*. And there was no money at all, not a sou –*all* had been spent for the funeral.'

The Countess was astonished. 'But that is true!' she said, 'that is exactly what had happened.'

Mildred wandered back, having got over her temper. She sat primly at the edge of the group, far from Robert, where she counted stitches and pretended to listen to the Countess with only half an ear.

'I don't suppose they grieved, not really,' Victoria continued. 'They hadn't known the grandmother at all – only her letters, and a photograph or two: an old lady, very stout, wearing her elegant *embriato* and sitting *te d'orato* in her garden under a lemon tree.'

The Countess shrugged, her beautiful mouth soured and drooping. ' – But it must have been a shock, nevertheless; death seemed to pursue them. And it was only too true for poor Nicky. Do you know how I found him? Distraught. Weeping. Alone. – He and his mother had rented the hot – a *bietetre*, really – in the slums. An artist

47

had built it as a studio; it was on a hill, the side of a cliff
– and it was a wretched place with a broken skylight
through which the rain was forever raining.'

'I can see it,' Mrs Carter said. 'I have a picture in my
mind.'

The Countess nodded, tears beginning to gather in her
eyes.

'One day. . . . I don't know quite how it happened
. . . Nicky said his mother had been shopping; she had
bought a quarter of a pound of *corte au dora* and a few
bones; she was going to make soup.'

'– With *corte au dora!*' Mrs Carter cried.

'– Yes; yes, it was that bad. But when she was climbing
the outside stairs – they were just stones, a few steps with
a rickety railing – she tripped' – Victoria paused, adding
quietly '– and plunged over the cliff to her death.'

The others were silent, watching the Countess who was
wiping the tears from her face and rubbing at the wetness
under her nose. She was caught in the memory and could
still see the *bietetre* – the grey rags that were curtains, the
tiny oil stove that clouded the room with a choking haze,
the police babbling away in their tireless Italian, and
heartbreaking Nicky, his tragic angel's face staring at his
mother, his cheeks streaming with tears.

'I buried her,' the Countess concluded.

She had been so moved by her account of little Nicholas
Passanante that her story would have ended there, but
many things seemed missing to Mrs Carter; the curtain
had come down much too soon.

'And then?' she persisted.

Victoria threw up her hands, taking heart.

'There was Nicky. – Should I have sent him back? He
had relatives in America; he could have gone to them.'
She shook her head quickly. 'But he was too sad, too beauti-

ful, too grieved. I fell in love with him. – With his grief, understand; with his sad beauty. I could not send him away. He became instantly too dear to me, too imperative. I could not eat. I could not sleep. I could not write a letter. I was filled with longing; I ached always to be with him. In the beginning, if he were out of the room, out of my sight for an instant, I suffered. I felt impoverished. He meant more to me than a lover; more than the first day, the first hour of love. Yes, he was like the dearest of pets, a sweet and beloved animal which somehow, in a special way, we always love so much more than human beings, and you know the anxieties *they* cause – because they are stupid somehow, and you worry constantly because you fear they are forever being run over by street cars, or mauled by other animals.'

She turned to the others with a penetrating gaze, looking directly at each in turn. '– Have you ever had an animal die – seen him killed, and picked him up and carried him in your arms? Don't ever do it – for you will be nearer to suicide than at any other time in your life. If you have a servant, send the servant to do it. Let him carry your dead animal away. Or a relative if one is near. Or a friend. Send a stranger if need be – pay a boy to do it; there are always small boys around when an animal dies. They come running. *Pay* him; *pay* him to do it!'

2

In their suite at the Polonaise, Paul Dier and his wife were lying peacefully in each other's arms, talking of Corbodéra and of Mrs Carter and her group.

Their peace at the moment was not the peace of immediately gratified love; it was the peace of depletion, of temporary physical exhaustion after weeks of almost incessant sexuality.

They had this day gone swimming late in the afternoon, avoiding Mrs Carter and the others gathered about her on the sand. They returned to the hotel and showered; then, cool and powdered, smelling of scented soap, desired to make love in their wide square bed as the incredibly blue and gentle twilight of Corbodéra settled over the island, seeming, like a quiet, windless fall of snow, to soften even the sounds outside their windows: the rhythmic crash of the surf, the hotel kitchen noises from below. and the eternal jazz from Nicky's short-wave radio that emanated from the Countess's suite down the hall.

They began the delicate, practised patterns of love, the gentle touches and breath-soft kisses, but knew, each of them secretly at first, that their bodies were emptied.

Paul sighed. There was the faintest of aches within him, a hunger so subtle, so remote that he hardly knew it existed. Suzette also sighed, and in a moment both were laughing, helpless and weak in each other's arms, content to enjoy the quietness, the novel peace of their sleeping passion.

The evening was warm, the louvres of their foyer door

opened wide, and through them came the increasing swell of Nicky's music as the boy, or the Countess perhaps, turned up the volume.

'Do you like it?' Suzette asked idly, kissing Paul's cheek.

'Not much,' he replied. 'Some. A little.'

'The French do. To them, there is nothing like American jazz.' She felt a slight chill despite the heat, and reaching down, drew up the sheet to cover both of them. 'I did not know much about it before the war. I was buried in Aix, which is quiet as you know, though I loved it. But during the war . . .' She turned, propping her head against an elbow that she might stare at Paul's profile silhouetted against the strange blue of the window. '. . . You Americans brought so many things that were new. You brought yourselves first of all, and nothing could have been newer and stranger to me.'

The silhouette smiled. ' "New!" ' it murmured, the tone as idle and drowsy as hers. 'When we are ten thousand years old, you Europeans will still refer to us as "new".'

'But you *are*,' Suzette insisted. 'Most Americans are not even awake; they are still sleeping in their cradles. – You have been lucky in your profession, I think. It has been like a hand on your shoulder shaking you, saying, "Wake up, open your eyes, look about you, you are alive!" ' She traced a gentle path across his profile with a forefinger. 'Most Americans – and you might as well admit it – are not individuals at all. They are all alike, all dreaming the same dream. Not even a war wakes them up; even that is swallowed in the dream. – I was a child during the last war, a girl – but your soldiers lived with us, many of them. I knew them. "What is America like?" I would ask; "Tell me what you miss, what you are break ing your heart to get back to." ' She paused, thinking. 'Do you know what it *was* most often – *Plumbing*; yes: bathroom fixtures, and huge refrigerators bursting with food; "sodas" at the corner drugstore, Sunday breakfast and Sunday comics. One soldier – oh, I was so shocked – actually told me he was fighting the war for the American Hershey Bar; all he wanted was to stand at the corner of Broadway and 42nd Street with a Hershey Bar in his hand. "That's living," he said.'

'He was joking,' Paul smiled. 'How could you have taken him seriously? He thought he was being funny.'

'I do not understand such humour.'

'But you understand – the Countess, for example. You appreciate *her* sense of humour.'

Suzette nodded, smiling. 'That's different. The Countess is very entertaining.' She sat up suddenly, looking down at Paul's face. '– Weren't you dying to laugh when she told about America?' She mimicked the Countess's deep sonorous voice: ' "I taught I vas on da moon." '

'It was very funny,' Paul agreed soberly.

'Well it was,' Suzette insisted. 'But serious, too. You must not think the Countess is amusing for the sake of being amusing. She has suffered. I'm sure she is suffering now with her beautiful, unrealisable Nicky.'

Paul sighed. 'But the American soldier had no capacity for suffering.'

Suzette was silent. She turned to look toward the window for a glimpse of the darkening sea.

'I suppose I am being unfair,' she replied. 'I do not know what the soldier felt, really. But who is to blame for that? Most Americans never *tell* you what they feel, or if they do, they tell you so obliquely, with so many idioms and peculiar American jokes, that you have to guess. They are worse than the English. When the world is crumbling before their eyes, all they can think of to wish for . . . is a bar of chocolate.'

' "Grief travels far," ' Paul said.

Suzette laughed. 'I kept wondering who "André" was. Perhaps I shall ask Mrs Carter.'

'I don't advise it,' Paul replied. 'Why not keep your illusions? I'm sure André will turn out to be a Siamese cat or a fawn-coloured parakeet. And that's carrying humour pretty far.'

'It is *not* humour,' Suzette insisted. 'It's . . . There should be another word, something that means crying and laughing at the same time, and seeing yourself as another person.'

'Schizophrenia,' Paul supplied.

'Oh!——' Suzette smiled in exasperation. 'The Countess is *fighting*. She hasn't, even yet, given up. That's what you don't see. She is saving herself. They all are – all the others, or some of them. Mrs Carter. Robert Hunter. Miss Hawkins lives for this summer on Corbodéra. She told me so. And when she told me, I thought she was describing a pilgrimage to Lourdes. It isn't that she expects a miracle. But for her the island, the summer, the sense of *belonging*, the fact that Mrs Carter really looks forward anxiously to seeing her each year – this is *her* salvation at the moment.'

Paul shook his head. 'Perhaps I don't see. Why are they saving themselves? For what?'

'Not *for*. – *From*.'

Paul shrugged. 'All right. *From* what, then?'

'What a silly question!' Suzette stared at him in silence for a moment. '– From death, of course. From age. From boredom and loneliness.' She paused. ' "Skilled music is lacking to our desire." – From constant . . . *reaching* for something that is never there.'

53

'It's there all right,' Paul said, and grabbed between her legs.

She gasped and pulled away, swinging a pillow down on his head.

'And you call yourself a psychiatrist! I pity your patients!'

'I'm sorry,' he laughed, and pinning her down, kissed her breathless.

'Stop it! Paul, stop it!' But she had to laugh, too.

Presently, when they were both quiet, he laced his fingers through hers. 'Now where were we? "Skilled music is lacking to our desire." – Who said that?'

'I don't know. Rimbaud, I suppose. Who else?'

Paul thought for a moment. 'His "skilled music" was his mother . . . the haunting, the *divine* Madame Rimbaud.'

'She troubled him always,' Suzette agreed.

'Things,' Paul said, quite seriously now, 'are frequently much simpler than we expect. We are dazzled by the variety and number and complexity of the *symptoms* a neurosis presents, but the root, if we are lucky enough to get to it finally, usually proves astonishingly simple. – As simple as a mother with a child in her arms – how she fed him, how she held him – the look on her face, in her eyes as she bathed him or wiped his behind.'

'Oh Paul!' Suzette frowned and laughed simultaneously. 'It isn't, it can't be as you say; not with Rimbaud, not with anyone. You don't believe it.'

Paul's face clouded. 'I not only believe it, I know it.'

'But Rimbaud——'

'He *wanted* his mother,' Robert insisted. 'He wanted to go back – dissolve, merge into that early experience. His "skilled music" was a memory of her body, her breast.'

54

Suzette thought about this, her bottom lip between her teeth.

'Then he was deluded,' she said finally; 'there is no "skilled music"– and never will be.'

Paul shook his head. 'There *is*. That is the whole point. It haunts all of us. It is something that never dies. But if, God help us, we are sufficiently wise to recognise, under-stand the impossibility of the wish – at least in part, then it doesn't kill us as it did Rimbaud. We go *on* writing poetry or painting pictures. We don't smoke hashish, or find a breast in a bottle of alcohol.'

Suzette returned, silent and still, to his arms. Presently she said: 'I understand some of what you believe, but' – she hesitated – 'there are times when you over-simplify. What you show me is a painting all in black lines, like a Rouault without all of the marvellous colour.' She paused. 'Sometimes I think there are *young* souls and *old* souls. The Countess, for example, is *very* old.' Paul was smiling. '–You think I am joking, but I am not. By the time Mozart was sixteen . . .'

'Oh,' Paul said, 'let's not go into *that*.'

'Very well. But one day you will find out things that all the psychiatry in the world cannot teach you. Wasn't it your beloved Freud who said that if he had another life to live, he might devote it to hauntings, and ghosts . . . psychic things?'

'– So?'

'Well . . . that is why you must not laugh. I saw you! You could hardly control yourself when Mrs Carter told us about Sleepy Waters. '

'*Sleepy Waters!*' Paul rolled away from her and then back, doubling up in laughter.

'And the visiting ichthyologist,' Suzette added; ' – do you remember that story the first day we met Mrs Carter?

. . . how the island would disappear because of the crabs?
Do you suppose it's true? – I mean that there really *was* an
ichthyologist who told her that? Or did she make it up?'

'I don't think Mrs Carter ever lies,' Paul replied. 'She
may exaggerate a bit, but I'm quite sure there really *was*
a visiting ichthyologist of some kind and that he actually
told her Corbodéra would sink – like "Atlantis or Mu"!
The wonder is that she believed a word of it.'

Suzette sat up again, leaning over Paul, her arms folded
across his chest. *'That'*s what I mean, too. You don't
really appreciate Mrs Carter, or any of the others. Even if
it weren't true, even if she made it up, like a story – don't
you see? She made it up for *you*, for *me*, and for the
others. And we were enchanted. She is an artist. She is
better than the best of circus clowns. And I applaud her!'

Paul was silent, smiling faintly. He put his arms beneath
his head, staring quietly at the sculptured cherubs, dancing and floating, smiling and posturing like idiots, around
the huge oval mirror opposite their bed.

3

'You have forgotten Heisenberg's Principle of Uncertainty,' Mrs Carter reminded the others, '– which states, if I remember it correctly, that nothing final can be known about anything. – Ever.' She thought about this for a moment; it seemed to puzzle her but she threw it off with a shrug. 'The ichthyologist explained that to me; you remember my telling you about the ichthyologist last year who came just after you had all left. He also told me about the Second Law of Thermodynamics. Why I remember – afterwards I was so angry because I had forgotten to ask him what the *first* law was. In any event, the second law means that everything is running down, the whole universe, you know . . . like a gigantic clock that has been wound up, but now there's no one to rewind it.'

'Who wound it in the first place?' the Countess inquired. Mrs Carter didn't speak for a moment.

'Well, I don't know,' she replied finally, 'I forgot to ask.'

'It was God who wound it,' Mildred announced dramatically, and a long silence followed.

'Certainly it would *seem* that way,' Mrs Carter said faintly. 'I can't imagine who else would do such a thing.'

A moment later she made a face. 'But that is anthropomorphic, and you will remember that we promised, *promised* each other not to be anthropomorphic this year.

'– At least we have gone *that* far,' she added, 'but everyone' – and she meant Mildred, of course, for having said thats God wound up the clock – 'is still talking about God as if He were human, a kind of . . . *magnified* man, with

57

all sorts of . . . *magnified* sensibilities. God is *not* human. Isn't that so, Robert? He is most *in*human.'

'I think you will find many people to agree with you,' Robert replied, smiling. He was dressed for a swim and seemed quite pale beside the others, most of whom, unlike him, were on the beach every day, soaking up the sun.

'There!' Mrs Carter said. She loved her small intellectual triumphs because they were so rare. The others at most times had a way of ignoring her, or smiling at her gently when she spoke of deep matters – as if they wanted to reach forward and pinch her cheek or pat her on the back of the hand.

'Don't you agree with me, Paul?' she asked, turning to the psychiatrist, of whom she had grown very fond.

'I'm afraid I don't have many opinions about God,' Paul replied. 'Though I must say He has proven very opinionated about me.'

It was a joke, apparently. Robert seemed to appreciate it, along with the Countess, so Mrs Carter joined in the laughter.

Everyone seemed in good spirits this morning, except Eduard Poussard who for the first time in more than a week – not since his argument about Picasso – had joined the group.

He was wearing his fishnet bathing suit and was wearing it, Mildred Hawkins felt sure, simply to irritate her, since he owned other, more suitable, suits. She had caught a glimpse of him swimming several mornings, sometimes at dawn, when he wore a modest if ridiculous pair of trunks that looked like faded dungarees that had been chopped off with a razor blade at the thighs.

She bided her time; then, pretending the sand was too damp where she sat, moved away from him, beyond Gia and Robert, who were now lying together on a blanket, but her eyes, despite her effort to control them, kept wandering back to the artist's trunks which were simply unbelievable, holding his male parts together like the net sack that holds oranges – and she could not understand why the others were not as offended as she. No one seemed to notice, however; or if they did, pretended otherwise.

The actress was almost as bad, her fantastically beautiful body – Mildred had to admit that – so meagrely covered with flesh-coloured nylon that if one looked quickly, or not too well, she appeared to be wearing nothing at all.

Between the two of them, Eduard and Gia, the beach for Mildred had turned into an American burlesque, or a French nightclub, with the kind of flagrant exhibitionism that she despised. Often in the mornings now, she stood at her hotel window chewing a fingernail, wondering whether to join the others or not.

Sometimes she didn't – preferring a solitary walk: a visit to Señor Gutiérrez and Evangelina, his small sweet daughter; perhaps a few moments in the church ruin to see if the *valdepeñas* had blossomed yet, or, if she brought her lunch and decided to cycle, a bit of shopping at Tanique, which was the small and only village at the south end of the island. It was usually deserted and rather depressing unless the fishing fleet was in, but it contained a small general store where she usually bought photographic supplies and a few colourful postcards to send to her favourite students.

Mildred's eyes returned to the artist, but this time she managed to keep them on the wide expanse of his handsome bronzed chest, his crew-cut hair and dark neat beard. He was good-looking, no doubt of that, but his sex, his maleness, clung to him like an odour, pervading the air around him. She could actually *smell* him, she thought – the smell of a sweating pig in the sun.

59

Robert, it seemed, was in splendid humour this morning – and this irritated Mildred, too. Obviously, he had been 'taken' by the actress – and went out of his way to talk to her – shyly, it was true – with slightly embarrassed smirks like a schoolboy. They even swam together, and there were an increasing number of 'private' jokes when he and Gia laughed at things they did not share with the others.

Even now as Mildred watched them, they were talking in low tones. It seemed ridiculous – a man of Robert's age and intellectual accomplishments, and she a cheap 'movie' person, a woman whose only talent was an exaggerated body which she allowed to be photographed in various stages of undress.

Robert and Gia swam presently, accompanied by Nicky, who couldn't get enough water, it seemed, though he could barely stay afloat and invariably brought the Countess knee-deep into the surf, shouting and gesturing wildly.

When they came back, Robert was in even better humour, smoothing his thinning hair into place to cover the beginning baldness on the top of his head, and rubbing himself dry with vigorous manly strokes as if his body were quite as robust as the artist's. There was a mischievous light in his eyes as he settled back on Gia's blanket and announced with a quick odd glance in Mildred's direction: 'I am writing a new novel.'

He had never written a novel in his life, and probably never would, since his profession was teaching and criticism.

Noting the look on his face, Mrs Carter decided promptly that he was in one of his 'silly' moods. He had, no doubt, thought up another of his wild plots to entertain them.

'Doesn't anyone want to hear about it?' he asked, peeved.

'But of *course* we do,' Mrs Carter replied. 'That is why we're quiet. We're waiting.'

Having secured their attention, Robert propped himself on an elbow.

'My novel,' he said, 'is about a beautiful young woman who, in many ways, has an ideal marriage; her husband *worships* her. . . .'

'I do love stories that begin that way,' Mrs Carter interposed, prepared to give him every advantage. 'Isn't it exciting?' She beamed at the others.

'They live in a small American town,' Robert continued, 'and the conflict involves a most *unusual* kind of trouble.' He paused. '– I think I shall call my heroine *Julia*.'

'*Excellent*,' Mrs Carter approved. 'It is a *lovely* name. I have always liked *anyone* called Julia. In Barcelona there was a salesgirl from whom I bought all my hats. Her name wasn't Julia, but she had a daughter – a tiny thing, who was lame, poor dear. I remember – every time I purchased a hat, I brought her an Italian ice. She was very fond of lime, though to me it had a dreadful colour. . . .'

She was aware that the others looked slightly pained. 'Do go on, Robert,' she instructed. 'Now be quiet everyone, please. I don't know what ails us this summer. There is always so much confusion.'

Robert returned to his story.

'Well, the trouble,' he said, 'the true *sine qua non* of the plot, is simply this. When Julia goes to the bathroom, her fæcal odours are *so* overpowering, so fantastically *awful*, that her husband is on the brink of a psychosis.'

A gasp of surprise caught Mrs Carter's throat. Robert's novels always had that effect upon her.

'There is nothing he can do,' Robert went on. 'Even when he is as far away as the garage, the odours have such a penetrating quality, they are so *ubiquitous*, so to

61

E

speak, that he hardly dares to breathe. He does wood-work, you know – in the garage; his hobby is carpentry and he is particularly skilled at making tie racks and shoe trees.'

Suzette Dier began laughing and could not control herself.

'I see instantly many of its symbolic levels,' Victoria Vranogrec-Markovici said with a straight face. 'It is sublimely Kafkaesque, and yet – how superior to anything the Austrian Jew ever thought. It has a certain . . . *la tietre de glasine*, or, as we say in my own language, *nava slav da borg.*'

'Yes,' Robert said. 'But let me go on. . . .'

The story ended there. Mildred Hawkins gathered up her knitting and without a word, but with a bored and sour expression on her face, moved twelve yards away where she sat herself down between two rocks and quietly re-sumed her knitting, though it was noticed that her hands were very rapid and her needles jabbed viciously at each other.

'Oh dear!' Mrs Carter said.

'She hasn't changed a bit,' Robert observed.

'But you are wrong to tease her so,' Mrs Carter repri-manded. 'I don't see how you can take pleasure in tortur-ing the poor girl. – Though I do admit I rather hoped she *would* change a little.' She looked at Paul Dier, explaining: 'Mildred is very sensitive on some subjects, as you can see. Wouldn't you think being with all those children all the time would get her *used* to things? She has the little tykes, of course, and I *know* it's the latency period, but I always wondered if Freud might not have been mistaken there. I seem to remember all *sorts* of vague sexual things going on when I was a child. In school children are always wanting to go to the bathroom in *pairs*; no sooner does one hand go up than there's another – or three or four, as if their kidneys were *synchronised* in some peculiar way. And I would hardly call *that* innocent. Of course, I never did witness anything personally. I was always *looking*, but I never saw anything really worth seeing. I think little boys have the advantage there. They stand *next* to each other. Little girls must go into cubicles all by themselves. I shouldn't wonder if that's what accounts for all the difference between the sexes – I mean, all this talk about woman's *natural* modesty. I don't think it's natural at all. If they weren't *conditioned* to weeing in those tiny dark cubicles, all alone, women would be flinging off their clothes at every opportunity. And *that*'s something Freud never thought of!'

She paused, glancing sadly toward Mildred.

'Robert, *do* apologise. See how lonely she is. Go and tell her you were only teasing.' But Robert refused. He settled comfortably back on the blanket, his hands beneath his head, his face to the sun.

'I don't know *what* you two have against each other, Mrs Carter continued. Suzette Dier was jerking with hiccups. 'Hit her on the back,' Mrs Carter instructed Paul, and then, turning to Robert: 'I suspect it's because you are very much alike, you and Mildred. You look at each other and it is like looking into a mirror at some deep level. And that's the truth. I have been with you too many summers not to know.'

She stopped because Robert was frowning, his bottom lip thrust forward like a sulking boy's.

4

Eduard Poussard's present canvas was seven by nineteen feet; much too large for any easel; he had nailed the canvas, unstretched, to a wall.

Staring at it as he so often did, Nicholas Passanante could see a bewildering pattern of colours – as amazingly complex as the frost he remembered on the window panes back home in Brooklyn. But unlike the frost with its arabesques of foaming lace, the artist's painting was composed of layered squares and triangles, more – at least in shape and texture – like the slivered sheets of mica he used to pick up from the stones by the East River. But it wasn't like mica, either; sometimes it seemed more like a trillion blue-green leaves raked into a disordered heap of nothing he could name. His throat felt queer, as if he were trying to form words, give shape to a phrase that would describe the painting. He ached to say, 'It's a forest!' or 'buildings that have fallen down!' or even 'a million coloured bottles that have been smashed against a sidewalk!' But it was none of these. It was nothing. Just a lot of crazy colours all mixed up and tangled together.

The artist never named it, perhaps taking it for granted that Nicky knew what it was.

He painted proudly, naked to the waist – usually in just dirty, paint-smeared shorts that had a hole in the back through which Nicky could see some hairs growing on Eduard's lower spine. And he painted with all sorts of dramatic movements, like an actor on a stage. Frequently he scratched his beard, or bit a knuckle, or held between his legs as if he had a pain down there.

When something pleased him in the canvas, he laughed as if he had painted a joke. Other times he would stand before it as though he was in a church when some holy words were being said. Once Nicky had seen him cry; yes – he had straddled a chair and stared long and quietly at the painting, the tears dripping from his beard. Nicky brought him a towel; the artist blew his nose in it loudly, and, seizing Nicky's hand, kissed it.

Surely this was the day to ask!

'What *is* it?' Nicky burst out, unable to resist a moment longer.

The artist turned to him in amazement.

'Do you mean to say you don't know what it is! – After all these weeks! It's the Sea of Corbodéra, of course! – Haven't you *seen* me looking out the window?'

Nicky nodded. He hesitated a long while, picking the dried paint from the end of a discarded brush. '– The sea doesn't look like that.'

'– But *feels* like that, eh?'

The boy's mouth hung open. 'What are these here?' – he asked, rising and pointing – 'these pink triangles.'

'*Don't touch!* – they're boats, of course. How can you be so stupid?'

The boy shut his mouth but continued to stare. 'The colour's pretty,' he concluded. 'It looks like linoleum. It looks like the kitchen floor my mother had back home.'

The artist threw up his hands.

'Why don't you *do* something?' he suggested. '– Clean my brushes.'

'They are clean. I finished them all last night.'

'Well – draw something then.'

65

The boy reached for a pad and a stick of conte. He sucked at the end of the crayon, pondering.

'What shall I draw?'

'The same stupid question! How many times must I tell you? Draw anything. Whatever you *like*. Whatever *appeals* to you.'

The boy bent over his pad and presently sketched a crude horse.

The artist looked at it.

'It's static,' he said, over-critically. 'The idea is to get some *life* into it. Everything you draw should have *feeling*. Something should be *happening*, something interesting and exciting.'

When the artist looked back a few minutes later, the horse was defecating, three scrawny big-eyed birds pecking at the manure.

He stared at the boy, his own mouth now hanging open.

'– Do you consider *that* interesting?'

'Well, it *happens* all the time,' Nicky defended. 'I used to visit a farm on Long Island . . .' He laughed but was obviously embarrassed and scratched out the drawing. 'Well – what else do horses make happen that *is* interesting?'

The artist shook his head in exasperation.

'That isn't the *kind* of happening I mean. It's not an *event* . . . a doing of something; it's what happens in the *lines*, the *shapes* of what you draw.' He gave up with a sigh.

Nicky was disheartened, but brightened quickly.

'I'll draw something pretty,' he said. 'I'll draw Vicky. Vicky sitting by the sea. She'll be looking at fishermen and boats. Only my boats won't look like yours. They'll be *real* boats.'

'A fine idea,' the artist said. 'A novelty.'

'What?'

'Nothing.' He kept staring at the boy. 'What do you do?' he asked presently. '– You and the Countess.'

The boy looked up, his eyes innocent.

'Do?'

'Yes. – Do you sleep together?'

Nicky didn't hesitate. 'Why no. I have my own bed. It would be too crowded. I have my own bedroom.'

The artist glanced down between the boy's legs at the small round bulge in his bathing trunks. Nicky caught the glance and his face turned pink as the meaning of 'sleep' became clear to him. He frowned, lowering his eyes.

'We don't do – *that*,' he said faintly. He tightened his lips, apparently quite angry at Eduard.

'Well, what *do* you do?' the artist asked, laughing and mussing the boy's hair.

'We don't *do* anything,' Nicky replied, his eyes still downcast.

'I'll bet you do,' Eduard persisted. 'I'll bet there's something you two do.'

'It's nothing,' Nicky said.

'Then there *is* something.'

'No. Only——'

'Come on. – We're friends, aren't we?'

The boy looked up quickly, anxiously. '– Oh yes!'

'Well then; tell me. Friends don't have secrets.'

'But it's nothing. It's just – she *looks* at me.'

'Where? What does she look at?'

Nicky was angry again, and just a little frightened.

'At *me*,' he said. '*Me*. I just – *sit*, and she looks at me. I don't know why. I thought it was funny at first. But it's nothing. And she wants to.'

'Every day? She looks at you every day?'

'Yes. I have to be there at eight o'clock – or whenever the twilight comes. It depends on where we are. In Rome the twilight came earlier than here. And then I sit – in a chair, or any place – near a window always – and she watches me until it's too dark to see.'

'And that's all?' The artist was looking at him as if he were lying.

'Yes,' Nicky said. 'She looks at me for about a half-hour or more. Until it's dark. She says – it's like a museum when she goes; like when she sits in front of a painting or a statue. She said once she sat for two months looking at some statue somewhere. *David* – some name like that. She brought her lunch and sat there every day, all day long. Only she says I'm better. – To look at. Better than this here statue.'

The artist stared at the boy's exquisite face.

'You are,' he said.

Nicky's bottom lip was thrust forward. '– She just likes to look, that's all.'

Eduard nodded. 'Yes. I believe you. And I understand.'

'What do you understand?'

'– Why she watches you. Why she looks.'

'Everyone likes to look. Everyone looks at me.'

'Do you mind? No – of course you don't. Think what it has brought you already.'

'What is that?'

'– A winter in Rome, a summer in Corbodéra. Fine clothes, good food.'

He was upsetting the boy. Nicky's face was troubled, his forehead lined.

'I know that. But why? I don't understand.'

'Someday you will.' Eduard paused, speaking to himself. '. . . And then you will become proud and vain and mannered and perhaps altogether silly. Or you may lose your fine looks. Maybe you're like a choir boy with an unbelievable, an incomparably fine soprano voice. One day it may just – *crack*. And then what? No one will want to hear you sing.'

'I don't – *sing*,' Nicky said.

'But you do,' Eduard smiled. 'Like the cherubim and the seraphim. God listens.'

'I don't know what you're talking about.'

'Do any of us?' Eduard inquired. 'We all make incomprehensible noises. It's a disease. And we're incurable. That's why I paint. – To speak without words. Tell me – why are you here? What is so – attractive about me? My room? – is that it? The good smells? – the turpentine and varnish? Or is it this . . . this piece of *linoleum* on the wall, with boats that don't look like boats. Perhaps it says something, eh? – perhaps it's saying something you like to hear.'

The boy was silent, and Eduard, looking at him, felt a moment's odd weakness. He wanted to reach forward, spread his hands wide and caress Nicky's head, know the reality of its weight and solidity, trace his fingers lightly across the nose, the mouth, infuse visual disbelief with the deeper, more convincing evidence of touch. And feeling this, his breathing became shallow, his heart seeming to pulse in his throat.

This from Eduard Poussard – a man without an inverted bone in his body. How often he had laughed at the fancy boys who, perfumed and plucked, cruised like a fleet through every European city he had ever known. No, that had never interested him much. Unless one counted . . . But he'd been in school then, hardly more than a boy himself. It was part of growing up. And he certainly didn't regret it. He had delighted in it. But there was so little finally, that one could really do with a man – and so much with a woman. It was a blind alley; one stewed in one's own juice.

'I'm busy,' he said suddenly. 'I've wasted an hour already. Either you stop bothering me or you get out. Don't think you can barge in here whenever you like just because you clean my brushes. And next time – remember – knock on my door before you come in.'

He was a little too rough in his tone. Nicky's face clouded; the lip came forward again, the eyes began to blink.

'And for God's sake, don't cry,' the artist added. 'You're too old for that. –A boy of your age!'

'You don't like me,' Nicky said.

'I *do* like you. I like you very much. – I'm teaching you to swim, aren't I? Look – come back after lunch and we'll go to the cove for another lesson.' He picked up a handful of brushes. 'Now go back to your Countess. She's probably looking for you.'

'She's not,' Nicky replied. 'She went to Tanique – with Paul and Suzette.'

'Well then – if you stay, you've got to be quiet.' He wheeled to face his canvas, spreading his legs and arms like a dancer who seeks renewed energy, a moment's intense, selfless concentration before beginning a difficult step.

'– Linoleum, you say,' he murmured. '– Which proves what fools children are.'

5

'SHE has just washed her hair,' Paul Dier said to the Countess, 'and is sitting on our balcony – like Rapunzel.'

'I admire your wife,' Victoria returned. 'We have talked several times.' She closed her book but kept a finger in place. It was not certain whether Dr Dier would sit down beside her on the veranda or join the others on the beach. He seemed dubious himself, but then, with a smile, settled in the chair next to hers.

'Where is Nicky?' he asked conversationally.

'– Ah, Nicky!' The Countess removed her finger from the book. 'He is with the artist, learning how to swim.' She had not yet, at least in Paul's presence, called 'the artist' by name. '– And I am sitting here pretending not to worry. Yesterday I watched, but my heart was in my throat. Each time I am tempted to forbid it, but it is giving Nicky much pleasure. And I can deny him nothing; there is nothing I would not give him.'

'Eduard is a fine swimmer,' Paul reassured her. 'I'm sure Nicky is safe.'

'Safe!' the Countess murmured. 'We live on the edge of doom, each with a yawning pit before him; one false step' – she snapped her fingers – 'and we topple in.'

The sound of laughter reached them; they both turned to glance at the group on the beach. Mrs Carter was making one of her rare excursions into the water but was doing so reluctantly and had to be coaxed and teased to the sea's edge by Gia Imola and Robert Hunter. Paul returned his gaze to the Countess and found her magnificent black eyes more melancholy than ever.

'I have a feeling about this summer,' she said darkly. 'I have a feeling about myself, and the others – all of you. I pretend it is nonsense but each day it grows stronger. Do you believe in such feelings, Dr Dier?'

Paul hesitated. 'I . . . *believe* in *all* feelings – since they exist, since they are real.'

'No, no.' Victoria shook her head. 'I mean, premonitions, intuitions.'

Again Paul hesitated. 'I have experienced a number of things that seemed prophetic.' He was about to go on but the Countess was impatient, waving him to silence.

'You are so cautious,' she complained with faint irritation. 'I'm not sure I have ever heard you express a truly robust opinion.'

Paul found himself piqued.

'You complain of a mysterious feeling of dread,' he said; 'you hint vaguely of impending disaster, and then you demand reassurance of some kind, though in what direction I'm not sure.'

'And neither am I,' the Countess returned, rather sadly. 'Of course you are right. "– A mysterious feeling of dread."' She sighed. 'That is about as well as I could have expressed it myself – in English. In my own language: *inchev borg*: it is another matter. But where do I feel the dread? – that is the question. Not in my head, or my heart. – In my entrails. That is precisely why it worries me. My head and my heart have been known to lie, but my entrails, never. When they speak – I listen; they have the authority of the infant.'

Paul smiled. 'The authority of the infant' – a curiously wise thing to have said – were it not connected with nebulous feelings of imminent disaster.

Victoria was thoughtful, caressing the leather binding of her book with a hand that was clustered with jewels, and the small silence and space between her and Paul seemed charged with her essence: a palpable richness, an age, a history and a decay that bore no relation to the time-now superficialities of her dimming beauty. He felt disturbingly young, crassly American, a new penny beside a Byzantine coin.

'Many things,' she said, '– the most important things, cannot be expressed at all; they are too subtle, too elusive for words. The eyes are good; a look, a glance tells much. A gesture is sometimes useful. If I love a man, I place fruit in his lap: several plums, a ripe peach, a handful of fine grapes. He understands.'

Paul laughed.

'What is so funny?' the Countess demanded. 'You do not agree?'

'Oh I do. Almost entirely. But tell me – what do you do when you hate a man?'

Victoria's expression clouded. 'It is not good when I hate. Once——' She hesitated. 'I will tell you. – Oh, but you would not believe it. Still – you are a psychiatrist. A psychoanalyst?'

'Yes.'

'Ah, so. And you have patients. They talk. All day long they tell you things. *This* you have not heard.'

Paul waited.

She moved her face close to his, her teeth clenched and bared.

'I have always had good teeth. Beautiful, no? Strong. Well, I held a razor blade between them – the kind with a single edge, the sharp side half an inch exposed.' She smiled as she settled back in her chair. '– He came to me as usual. The room was dark, my hands were tender. I

73

held his head gently as he bent to kiss me. – And cut his mouth to ribbons.'

This he had not heard.

'I was twenty-two at the time,' Victoria added, staring toward the sea, 'and not particularly imaginative. Today' – she looked up at him obliquely – 'I would put the razor blade somewhere else.'

With this she laughed in her explosive, ribald way, and rising, crossed to the balcony where she stood with her back to him. When she turned once more, it was the haunted melancholy Victoria who did so, the great brooding eyes swinging in a slow arc until they found him, and seized him.

Amazing woman! He felt locked in her gaze; it was more intimate than being touched.

'But enough of love and hate,' she said. 'Are you enjoying Corbodéra?'

6

'VIOLETS are my favourite spring flower,' Mrs Carter said.
'But they are a sad flower. They always remind me of
Shakespeare. One of his plays, you know.'

Mildred Hawkins who was on her knees beside the older
woman helping to weed the *avezia* bed at the side of the
hotel, could not see the connection. She sank back on her
heels with a bewildered look.

'Well, they are a *small* flower,' Mrs Carter explained.
'Fragile – like all of us. And their colour is a tragic one,
too strong, too rich for their tiny size. Don't you see?
They seem to carry a burden they can hardly bear – like
Desdemona.'

Mildred's face cleared somewhat.

'Also,' Mrs Carter continued; 'they are sold in *bunches*.
One wouldn't dream of buying a single violet, would one
– as if they were always lonely and had to be with others.
For this reason, I have always considered them a *social*
flower.'

She returned to her weeding, adding between breathless
pauses: 'I remember – I once wrote a paper to that effect.
I was president of the African Violet Society of Greater
New York at the time, and I must say . . .'

Mildred had arranged an attentive, sober expression on
her face, but Mrs Carter was much too acute an observer
to be fooled by it.

'You're laughing at me!' she accused good-naturedly,
and in the next moment both were hysterical.

'*Surely* it was better than bird-watching,' Mrs Carter

gasped. 'And I did . . . do that . . . for a while. But I was always seeing birds that weren't there – at least no one else ever saw them. I don't know *how* many times I sent my whole club – ninety-two members, understand – rushing off into the underbrush. You know how the underbrush *moves*; it is *always* moving in some mysterious way, and I expect that is the reason why I kept seeing strange colours and flashes of wings. My bird book was usually completely filled – every specimen checked off – before the others could even turn a page in theirs. You can't *imagine* how jealous it made them! . . .'

She had to pause to abandon herself to a fresh explosion of laughter, adding almost incoherently: 'Bird-watchers are among the most envious persons alive. – And what are they, after all – platonic Peeping Toms, spying mercilessly on all those small private creatures. I'm sure I'm right. I shall have to remember to ask Paul what a bird means. . . .'

They were again laughing so hard that finally Mrs Carter had to beg Mildred to stop. 'I shall become ill,' she choked; 'it is not good for my heart.'

The girl made an effort but the laughter had seized her, flinging her body backward across a border of the scarlet *avezia*. As she covered her mouth trying to stifle the sounds, the laughter drained from Mrs Carter's own body. She realised Mildred was crying.

Astonished, she simply sat there and stared until she had the presence of mind to lean forward and touch the girl's hand.

'My dear, my dear,' she whispered; 'what is it; why are you crying?'

It was some moments before Mildred could control herself; she then struggled to a sitting position, wiping the tears from her stained face. She glanced at the bruised

76

avezia where her body had sprawled. 'Look what I have done!'

'We'll give them a little water,' Mrs Carter promised. 'They'll spring back presently; they are a hardy bloom.' She was silent, waiting.

Mildred dabbed at her eyes once more, and brooding, twisted an *avezia* petal around one finger.

Mrs Carter smiled.

'I have my deeper side, you know,' she offered shyly. 'I am not altogether the frivolous woman I appear. I . . . *buy* my way, so to speak. It passes the time; it attracts people.'

It was a time for honesty, apparently.

'I haven't laughed, really laughed, in so long,' Mildred said wistfully.

'– Nor cried, I imagine. I envy you. I am capable of the laughter, but not of the tears. I buried two of my husbands and did not cry. I have not truly cried since my father died, and that was – thirty years ago. Unless one counts – physical pain. I had a boil once – I shan't say where – that made me cry for two days straight. But the other kind——' She shook her head.

'I had no *reason* to cry,' Mildred said with a slight tremulous intake of breath.

'One doesn't cry for *reasons*,' Mrs Carter replied. 'Reasons belong to the head, not to the heart.'

'But——'

'One cries, I imagine, for exactly' – she laughed – 'the same *reason* a child cries: because he's denied something he wants desperately, or because he has lost something . . . something beautiful and precious, something dear.'

Mildred was confused and full of protest. She threw up her hands. 'But I have lost nothing!' she said, and – so

77   F

characteristic of women – glanced down at her lap – as if it might have been quite full of whatever it was that Mrs Carter was intimating she had lost.

The time for honesty was over.

7

WHEN Eduard was not looking, Nicky dared to glance at him quickly, carefully between the legs.

How fine! he thought. How beautiful! – Like a strong white bird asleep in its nest. – It always swung when he walked, leaped and bounced when he ran or jumped or dived from the rocks. Only when they came out of the water, if they had stayed too long, was it tight and small, sometimes puckered and white like the tips of their fingers.

His own, at moments like these when it was necessary to compare it with Eduard's, seemed pathetically small: a week-old chick beside a great strutting rooster.

But one thought was comforting: Eduard was a man; he was really very old – maybe thirty-five or forty, and all that time his had been growing, while his own had been alive barely fourteen years and only in the last two or three had it increased appreciably and satisfyingly in size.

One day, Nicky promised himself; yes, one day, and very soon, his own would be big: bigger than Eduard's, bigger than his father's which he remembered so vaguely and had seen only once or twice. Perhaps it would be the biggest in the world. – Only that might be a bother – you know? – keeping so much of it in his trousers all the time?

– They were lying naked on the sand, panting after a swim, and Eduard had spread himself out as shamelessly as the dead. But he was aware of every inch of his nakedness – and of Nicky's too. To ignore it, to pretend not to look, not to know and to share their mutual interest and pleasure, was to Eduard a sickness. His display, always, was a lesson for the boy who, for the first time, seemed ready to respond. Today he seemed more modest than shamed, and instead of lying on his stomach as he usually did, relaxed comfortably on his back. His legs were bent, the knees up, but gradually the leg nearest Eduard lowered to the sand.

Had the boy had no father? Eduard wondered – no one to say to him, life is good, the body is good, your flowering manhood most beautiful, most pleasurable to see?

Look and be looked at; be relaxed, be warm, be comfortable and unafraid. Eduard strained his feeling toward the boy as if it were as communicable as words.

And perhaps it was. Nicky's eyes were closed, but he was not sleeping. There was a faint smile on his lips, and the muscle of one cheek kept moving in a tiny spasm.

And as Eduard watched, the boy's skin tightened in a rash of instant gooseflesh, then smoothed again, as if a sudden brief wind had roughened the surface of the sea. A moment later, Nicky was laughing – a small funny sound – and stretching himself sensuously.

The boy's whole body must be aching with the sweetness of its own secret living: it was a flower, growing, expanding, opening before his eyes. And with every strength in him, Eduard endorsed, selflessly adored each fragile petal that unfolded.

Nicky rolled over on his stomach, lifting his shy, smiling eyes to Eduard's. They were touched with delight and humour.

The artist's own smile deepened, and he smiled at the boy for many moments before he spoke.

'It's time for a last swim. After that, I must return to

the hotel. I haven't touched a brush all day. God will never forgive me.'

Going back, Nicky walked laughingly behind Eduard, stretching his legs wide, stepping carefully into each footprint the man was making in the sand.

8

'I NEVER knew anyone who owned one,' Robert Hunter said. He was lying face down on Gia's blanket, soaking up the sun.

'I didn't *own* one,' Mrs Carter replied. 'There was some law by then prohibiting their sale. They could not be shipped across the state line – that was it.' She removed her sunglasses to look at him. 'I'm not sure I would have bought one anyway, since, as I told you, my sister had an excellent one and I could sit in it whenever I liked.'

'He was a brilliant man,' Paul said. 'A pity.'

'And did you?' Gia inquired of Mrs Carter.

The actress was applying suntan lotion, and stood before the others rubbing the oil into the long smooth muscles of her thighs until her beautiful legs glistened. She did this with sensuous concentration, pulling up her nylon suit to expose half moons of glittering white buttocks.

'– Did I what?' Mrs Carter asked.

'Sit in the box.'

'Well, of course. Many times. Completely nude. I believe *some* light clothing is allowed, but to me it seemed like putting a duck into the oven with all its feathers.'

This brought an explosion of laughter from the others – at least from Robert and Paul and Mildred; the Countess, who had forgotten her glasses, had her nose two inches from a book, and Nicky, oblivious to everything but his play, was building a sand castle.

Gia remained thoughtful and mystified.

'But——'

82

She continued her massage, cupping a hand for more of the thick golden liquid from her bottle. Now she turned to her shoulders and arms with equal devotion.

Mildred, who was knitting blindly as usual, could not take her eyes from the actress. Surely the woman was ill with a morbid love of her own flesh, a diseased pride in her own body. Yet this very sickness and pride had produced – to Mildred's bewilderment – a magnificently healthy physique. No body could have appeared more vital, more alive, more poised for action or repose.

'But what *happens*?' Gia asked, her puzzled eyes still on Mrs Carter.

'Happens? – When you sit in the box?'

'Yes.'

The older woman shrugged. 'Nothing – *dramatic*. You gather the orgone. The box is simply a device to concentrate it; isn't that true, Paul?'

Paul inclined his head politely, smiling with his usual ambiguity.

'I must defer to one who has had the experience,' he replied.

'*What* experience?' Gia insisted. 'You said nothing happens.'

'Well nothing *ordinary*,' Mrs Carter answered. She was perplexed and found herself redundant. 'You simply gather – the orgone.'

'Why do you do that?'

Mrs Carter sighed. 'Because it is *good* for you, my dear.'

Paul had been watching the actress as closely as Mildred, marvelling at Gia's healthy, innocent, and to him completely unselfconscious narcissism. Self-love, self-regard, he reminded himself, was the basis of an expansive, embracing world love. It began with the body. Psychiatry had been forced to an operative dualism, a pragmatic 'as if' because a dichotomy presented itself in the neurosis. Each organ had a 'psychic' counterpart. There was a physical stomach, and a psychic stomach, a biological, physiological penis and a spiritual penis. The ulcer, for example, began as a morbid condition of the 'psychic' stomach; male impotence, more obviously, as 'spiritual' self-castration. But in the healthy, completely at-one-with-its-environment man or woman – if such existed – all separation seemed to disappear, the 'self', physical, mental, spiritual and environmental, functioned as a unified, inseparable whole.

Robert, who was still lying on his stomach, his head on his hands, sat up suddenly to announce with his sometimes irritating I-know-everything, just-ask-me air: 'Orgone is alleged to be a universal non-electric magnetic force . . . comparable to the energy of physics; as the basis of sexuality, it is Freud's id in a bio-energetic form.'

All of which meant absolutely nothing to Gia.

'*Precisely*,' Mrs Carter agreed, wishing that Robert wouldn't be quite so much of a show-off. 'And it is in the atmosphere, you know; it is everywhere – apparently as immanent as Tao. Or do you know the Indian *prana*? – it is more like that. One gathers prana, too. And quite without a box – or any mechanical device whatsoever. Which *proves* how superior the Orientals are in these matters. Why we cannot import a simple spiritual idea like prana without interpreting it in plywood and steel and supposing it can be trapped in a few and I must say very mysterious dimensions is more than I can understand. It is rather like the Catholics – they keep their God in a box, too – as if God could be *concentrated* – like instant coffee.' Her breath caught and she covered her mouth quickly with a frightened glance at Mildred, but the girl was flashing her needles and seemed in no way offended.

Reassured, Mrs Carter reminded herself that Mildred was no longer a Catholic – though sometimes she had to wonder if the vestigial effects hadn't remained. Once last summer, Mildred had risen at three in the morning and paid Señor Gutiérrez thirty dollars to sail her to the mainland for Sunday Mass. She seemed to have been in some sort of emotional distress at the time and had been mooning for days beforehand, blushing and stammering if one so much as asked her to please pass the sugar.

'And how does one gather – what is it now? – the prana?' Gia asked.

'By breathing,' Mrs Carter revealed instantly. 'Simply that. Breathing.' Her chest rose strongly. 'One breathes it subtly, purely. One thinks of the air as silvered, richly composed. It refreshes and revitalises. Or——' she stopped her breathing abruptly '– one can gather it by merely waving one's hand through the air. Like this. – Try it.'

Gia imitated Mrs Carter's rhythmic hand movement.

'I feel nothing,' she said.

'Well you must *practise*,' Mrs Carter returned severely. 'One does not play a violin the very first time one picks it up.'

Nicky, too, tired of his sand castle and having heard part of the conversation, now began waving his hand through the air.

'I feel it!' he cried. 'It's coming in my hand.'

The Countess, who had not listened to the theory of the orgone, preferring the last pages of her detective novel, was shaken from her myopic concentration by Nicky's cries.

'*What* is coming in your hand?' she demanded, looking up.

No one bothered to answer her, and in the next moment

she had forgotten she had asked. The setting sun behind Nicky's head had outlined his profile in fire.

Mrs Carter followed Victoria's transfixed gaze and misinterpreted it, imagining the Countess to be staring at the sun. She herself looked and her arms became covered with gooseflesh. For the third time in two weeks she had what she now called 'that feeling'. There *was* something strange about Corbodéra's sun. There was something strange about Corbodéra this summer. She glanced from the sun to the water – where Gia and Robert were now splashing – and then to the smoky blue chalk cliffs in the distance. The twilight was already there, crowding toward them across the sand, more fog than shadow. And as she looked, the cliffs seemed to tremble, but tremble so slightly that vision, *per se*, was useless. She *felt* the cliffs tremble – as if, too small, too fine for translation into literal sight, minute nerves in the retina of her eyes had begun to vibrate.

'Robert!' she called sharply. 'Robert Hunter!' – but he was beyond earshot. She turned back. 'Victoria – see there! *That* is what I tried to explain the other day. – The cliffs! Do look quickly; it lasts only a moment.'

But before the Countess found the strength to take her eyes from the boy – it *was* the boy, not the sun – the tremble had disappeared.

9

THE ice-cream, on arrival, proved to be a thick semi-frozen sherbet made of evaporated milk and bitter with oil of lemon. Bright, almost greenish yellow, it appeared even more ghastly under the store's flickering neon light.

Nicky's first thought when he saw it was of melted snow – over which a dog had lifted its leg and peed copiously.

Suzette spooned it doubtfully, ventured a taste, then with a wry face at Paul decided she'd rather live – at least a while longer. Paul had more courage, managing to down a few mouthfuls. Nicky proved bravest, or most foolhardy. He tasted his, sighed with almost tremulous disappointment, but then cleaned his dish, belching loudly and concluding, 'That was awful.'

He left their table to eye the coke machine. It was covered with dust; a spider had spun its web over the bottle opening. There was a juke box, too, a garish monster, against one wall, but its insides were busted, every record smashed, as if all its internal machinery had exploded. He squinted through the discoloured milky glass at the broken records to see if he could read the song titles. One fragment said, 'Love', and another one said, 'Love'.

He walked to the rickety food bar, fingering a sweaty coin.

'You got any root beer?'

The fat man had a gold tooth and hair as black and shiny as liquorice. One round ear-ring glittered.

'Si, si.' – Grinning, bobbing his head.

Nicky repeated the question. '– You know; root beer.'

He lifted his hand, an imaginary glass to his mouth.

'*Si, si.*' – Bowing, nodding, the dark face wrinkled with pleasure.

Nicky drained the greasy glass of water he was offered and pocketed the money.

Suzette and Paul were waiting out of doors. The day had remained a white fire, shadowless, the sun a weight on their shoulders. There were big wet circles under Paul's armpits, a streak down the middle of his back, and a dark triangle in his crotch. Suzette was dressed lightly, but her sweat was long tears inside her arms, the fine hair at her temples stuck to her skin – as if she had just come from swimming.

It was two miles back from Tanique and they stood limply together, waiting for the courage that would set the wheels of their bicycles in motion.

Paul glanced toward the empty boat wharfs, following Nicky's gaze.

'Another time,' he promised, touching the boy's shoulder. '– When it's cooler.'

'They're coming in now!' Nicky said, his eyes lifted to the horizon.

'I think they are,' Suzette agreed.

But it was only a flock of Corbodéra's flaming *estrollata*.

They stopped twice on the way while Nicky supplied them with handfuls of a dark sweet berry which Señor Gutiérrez had taught him was edible, and soon their mouths were blue-black with the fruit's winy juice. He inspected Suzette's tongue with lavish interest; next, Paul's, which he ventured to touch; then he stuck out his own tongue. They agreed his was the best – blackest of all.

Watching him, listening to his shouts of laughter, Paul realised that this was not the same grieved, withdrawn boy the Countess had brought to the island.

She had changed him apparently. Or Eduard had – with his rough affection – and daily swimming lessons.

They stopped at Señor Gutiérrez's *benita* for a glass of cool water, but neither he nor Evangelina was home.

'See if a screen is unlocked,' Suzette begged. She was dying of thirst.

They prised one loose and Paul boosted Nicky up to crawl through the small opening. He unlocked the front door and, in the tiny dark kitchen, they pumped water and drank until they thought they would burst.

'It has a peculiar taste,' Suzette said with a frown. 'I noticed it at the hotel, too. Mrs Carter is right. Something is happening to Corbodéra.'

'Like what?' Paul inquired.

'Well I don't know. But even this heat. Robert told me that during all the summers he spent here, the temperature was never above eighty.'

'It must be a hundred now,' Nicky said; '– or two hundred.' He gulped his fifth glass of water.

Suzette took the glass from his hand. 'You'll be sick. Your stomach will explode.'

Nicky laughed, picturing his erupted stomach spewing forth in a torrent, filling the room, the house, carrying Paul and Suzette down the road in a river.

They returned to their journey and by the time they had reached the church ruin, Nicky had to go to the lavatory so badly he could barely get off his bike.

'I told you not to drink so much!' Suzette scolded.

'Go there,' Paul said, pointing. 'Behind that wall.'

'In the church!' Nicky replied, scandalised.

'God won't mind. – He's used to such things.'

Nicky disappeared shyly, and presently they heard the hiss and splatter of his urine against the loose stones. It

89

was much louder than necessary and seemed to go on interminably.

'I could go myself,' Suzette said, listening.

'Then go,' Paul advised. 'You're next.'

'No, I'll wait,' Suzette replied. 'It's only another ten minutes.' But hearing Nicky made her want to go all the more. When the boy came back – hitching up the short pants the Countess liked him to wear though he was much too tall for them – she disappeared behind the wall.

She didn't make a sound, though Nicky strained to hear. He glanced at Paul, wondering why he didn't have to go too. It was exciting – all this public peeing.

Suzette returned, her skirt covered with burrs. Nicky pulled them off, wincing and ouching and sucking elaborately at his fingers.

They couldn't leave without inspecting the *valdepeñas*.

'Mrs Carter would never forgive us,' Suzette said, though it was obvious she wanted to see it herself.

So they moved to the far side of the ruined altar, stumbled down the rock-strewn slope. There, shining with health, magnificently thick with foliage, its broad bottle-green leaves spread flat and wide in the sun, not one shadowing the other, grew Corbodéra's notorious *valdepeñas*.

Its single bud, waist-high, at the very centre of the plant and surrounded by smaller darker leaves that were almost black, was larger than a man's fist, and had the strong clenched appearance of a man's fist. It was so full, so ripe that it seemed ready to open and flower before their eyes, and they stood silent, staring at it, half-expecting the happy event to occur as they watched.

But nothing happened and Suzette sighed her disappointment. It was the third time in a week she had

90

stopped to see the *valdepeñas* – once with the Countess and the other time with Mildred Hawkins.

Paul said, 'Come on.' The *valdepeñas* bored him; he didn't share the interest the anticipated flowering generated in the others. 'It will probably be a monstrosity anyway.'

'It's sweating!' Nicky cried. 'Look at that!' – for he had discovered a globuled sheen of moisture on several of the lower leaves.

'Even the plants sweat,' Paul remarked, wiping at the beads of moisture dripping from his chin. If the road had been hot, the church ruin was unendurable; the heat, pocketed between walls, had gathered in a vast still pool.

'Perhaps that's why it's blooming this year,' Suzette said.

'You mean the heat?' Paul inquired.

'Yes. Perhaps every seven years or whatever the time is, there is a sunspot, or an unusual climatic change of some sort – causing the heat, which in turn makes the flower bloom.'

'My God,' Paul said; 'you sound like Mrs Carter.'

'Well, there has to be *some* reason,' Suzette replied.

'Of course there's a reason,' Paul returned, a little impatiently. 'Plants have flowering cycles. There are annuals and perennials, and plants that bloom the second year, and the seventh. Now come on. It's not going to pop open before your eyes.'

'Why don't we cut it off and take it home?' Nicky asked. 'We could put it in water and watch it all the time, every minute.'

Suzette was horrified. 'Don't you dare! Mrs Carter would never forgive us. We must wait. We must wait patiently.'

Paul stared curiously at his wife. She seemed to have become as infected as the others with a kind of *valdepeñas* madness. – All this stupid excitement because some un-classified giant weed was about to flower!

He was half-way to the road. 'Come on!' he shouted. 'Both of you.'

They followed him out of the ruin but Suzette actually stopped twice to stare back.

'It *is* beautiful,' she said, as they picked up their bicycles. 'And exciting somehow. There's really something about the plant that . . .'

She didn't finish. Paul was looking at her severely, with a puzzled diagnostic gleam in his eye. And *that* from a husband, particularly one who is a psychiatrist, closed her mouth firmly.

10

'THERE are blood banks,' Mrs Carter said to Paul Dier.
'– And bone banks. – And eye banks. And now, I am told,
they are thinking of starting a sperm bank.'

Paul was tempted to tease Marion. Who – are 'they'?
he wanted to ask – the mysterious, ubiquitous 'they' who
kept her so well informed. He had never seen her read a
newspaper, not once in his presence had she opened a
book or a magazine, there were no radios on Corbodéra
except Nicky's, and yet 'they' kept her in constant supply
with all kinds of fascinating news, even of their most
esoteric activities.

'They have discovered,' she continued, 'that it can be
quick-frozen and remain in perfect condition for hundreds
of years.'

She sighed with pleasure.

She and Paul were enjoying one of their relaxed 'alone'
moments together, though she had wondered an hour ago,
when he'd refused to join his wife and the others in their
walk along the beach, if he hadn't some special reason for
wanting to remain with her. Later, she decided that it was
simply their 'time'. Civilised, sensitive man that he was,
he found time for aloneness with everyone. She had seen
him chatting with the Countess, and with Robert on occa-
sion, and with Mildred, and Nicky. She knew he even
visited Eduard, but in the studio – since the artist could
so rarely leave his painting to join the others without
pangs of guilt.

'Of course,' she went on, 'it won't be like our blood

banks; they're not *looking* for donors. What I mean is – they don't want just *anyone's* sperm; no, there wouldn't be much point in that, would there, considering the unlimited supply. What they want, naturally, is sperm from men of genius. Take Einstein. Think what it would mean if we had a supply of *his* sperm.'

She paused, giving Paul time to think, but nothing of any particular significance occurred to him.

'What *would* it mean?' he asked.

'Why the theory,' she answered, surprised, 'is that one day we will be able to create geniuses at will – we will be able to adjust the demand and supply, to to speak. For example. If we are *low* on brilliant' scientists at some sociological time or other and need a few men of really exceptional talent to stimulate the age, why we can go to our bank, find Mr Einstein's sperm, and then – by thawing it out or whatever it is they do to activate it – impregnate through artificial insemination tens or even hundreds of suitably healthy and eugenically *correct* young women.'

Paul nodded sagely. 'I see,' he said. But it was evident he did not see at all, not at all. 'And after we have impregnated all these eugenically correct young women? . . .' he asked.

Mrs Carter threw up her hands.

'Foolish boy! Why we wait; we simply wait. Naturally, each of these women will produce at least *one* baby, and because *all* have been sired, in effect, by a man of manifest genius, the law of statistical averages indicates . . .'

'The what?' Paul interrupted.

'The law of . . .' Mrs Carter looked at him over the top of her glasses. 'Why are you smiling at me that way? Surely you know that everything is statistical these days; even truth. It all started with dice, I believe, and the laws of chance – though that is one thing I thought very odd –

that there should be *laws* of chance. It seems to me that if chance were really chance, there couldn't possibly be any laws governing it at all. There would be sheer chaos. – Or am I being stupid?' She shrugged. 'In any event, I am fascinated by the whole idea – the sperm bank, that is. And don't tell me you aren't.'

Paul laughed. Being with Marion, no matter what they talked about, always gave him pleasure.

'Very well, I am fascinated,' he replied. 'But also doubtful. Men of genius frequently produce quite ordinary sons and daughters.'

'That,' Mrs Carter returned promptly, 'may be environmental. To be reared by a man of genius is to be staggered by his accomplishment. One refuses to compete; indeed, it is very discouraging. One's ideal, the image to which one aspires, is too monumental.'

Paul shrugged. There was something – if not very much – to that.

'So we produce – what we need,' he concluded. '– What the age needs. But who will decide?' He smiled at her again, and it seemed to Mrs Carter that his smile was just a bit crooked. '– Will *they* decide that?'

She looked at him blankly.

'They?'

Paul laughed again. 'Yes. *Who* will decide? Take our own age. How luckless to imagine we need artists if what we truly need is mathematicians. Perhaps we will breed a particular *kind* of genius who will decide what *kind* of genius the age lacks.'

The momentary silence between them had the quality of silence that usually follows a very stupid remark. Mrs Carter glanced away and then back at him, finally giving him the benefit of the doubt.

'Nonsense!' she replied. 'Everyone knows what our age

95

lacks. We suffer from a plethora of scientists. And that is the truth. They are the source of our anxiety. Never mind the corrupt politicians; it is the scientists – with their blackboards and chalk – who put the weapons in our hands. All those innocent hieroglyphics! What we need so sorely today is men of religious genius – *psychological* genius, if you will – through whom we can balance this dreadful excess of physical knowledge.'

The others were coming back; Suzette and Nicky, hand in hand; the Countess and Mildred behind them, followed by Gia and Robert who, together, were carrying a huge piece of driftwood.

'And that is why,' Mrs Carter rushed on, anxious to conclude before the others arrived to interrupt her, '*I* am in favour of the sperm bank. I may even endow it if it comes to that. – Though I feel – what a pity, what a *great* pity, it couldn't have been started years, even *centuries* ago. If it had, just think, Paul – *I* might have borne Socrates' child. Or a son to Moses! Amenhotep! Why I have only to close my eyes to *see* all those bottles – or tubes – covered with frost and labelled *Zola! Spinoza! Raphael! Beethoven! Bach!* Not to mention' – and she leaned forward in sudden ecstatic triumph – '*Freud!*'

Part Three

I

'WHAT did you find in your milk today?' Nicky asked.

'An old mouldy shoe,' the Countess replied; 'my grandfather's gold false teeth.'

'An old mouldy shoe!' Nicky chided with grins and smirks; 'your grandfather's . . .'

Vicky was never a challenge; she always laughed right away when Nicky was Milkman.

'What did you find in your milk today?' he asked Mildred.

She was a tiny bit drunk, having accepted the glass of *obala* Eduard had offered her during dinner. It was the first time the others had ever seen her drink.

'Well?' Nicky asked. '–What did you find?'

She was dreamy-eyed and widely smiling.

'A garland of roses,' she replied airily; 'some fairy lace; an enchanted mushroom. . . .'

It was too much for Robert. He picked up his glass and moved deeper into the shadows of the veranda.

'What colour were the roses?' Nicky asked slyly.

'– A garland of roses,' she chanted; 'some fairy lace; an enchanted mushroom.'

'What kind of lace?' – Grinning, screwing up his face, sticking out his tongue.

'A garland of roses . . .' But then she went weak with silly laughter, her body hanging over her chair like a doll's.

He turned to Gia. Her body was steel, her face a stone mask.

99

'What did you find in your milk today?'

It was the first time she had played the game and the effort to control herself and not to laugh made the pulse in her throat throb visibly.

'A pizza,' she answered between beautiful clenched teeth; '– *two* pizzas, one anchovy, one cheese.' And then the laughter moved up through her body like a wave in the sea, crashing over Nicky's head. In the next moment she had caught him in a bear hug, whirling him dizzy, the sounds of her childish delight like bells and tambourines in his ears.

2

'. . . And it is, as ever, breathtaking,' Mildred wrote. 'The weather has turned unexpectedly warm – so unlike Corbodéra! – but the sky is as blue and the sea as beautiful. So it's hard to explain; it must be me, as usual. You know my spells; not my ear this time; at least that's behaving! –but my headaches have returned and I don't sleep well. This morning I was up at dawn, walking the beach.

'Dreadful Nicky was bathing – *sans* trunks, and this is the second time I've caught him. Once more and I shall do something about it. Heaven knows, I'm no prude, but he isn't exactly a child, you know; he's an adolescent, with the unmistakable signs of adolescence, and a little modesty would become him.'

Mildred paused, clicking the end of her pen against her teeth. She re-read the last sentence and underlined 'little modesty'.

'I'd be the last to imply anything nasty, but you do see – a woman of her age – living with a fourteen-year-old boy! Of course, he's an *orphan*, he's *destitute*, but I can assure you her feelings are something more than motherly, though what their precise relationship is I haven't been able to discover. The only thing I can get out of Nicky is a moronic grunt or a monosyllable, and Victoria, for all her likeable qualities, is so completely affected, so 'posed' and 'unreal' that it would take a psychiatrist to determine what is genuine.

'Speaking of psychiatrists, I find I adore Dr Dier – "Paul" I should say, because that is what I call him. His wife, too, is a joy – so wholesome and plain, and they, at least, along with Marion who is her usual charming self, are making my summer bearable.

'You asked about the *valdepeñas*. Well, it *still* hasn't blossomed! We are *dying* of curiosity and have arranged *relays* to keep it under constant surveillance. Every day one of us visits the church ruin and returns with a *detailed* report on its condition. (It's like waiting for a blessed event!) Cross your fingers that I will be the first to see it.

'*Status quo* with Robert Hunter and the "actress". He is still simpering and drooling and I won't bore you with the juvenile details. Do you suppose they'll be "sleeping" together before the summer is over? Perhaps they are even now. Though truly I couldn't care less. I'm merely puzzled. What *happens* to men of that age? And a man of his *intellectual* pretensions. You should see her. Sex personified – *so* exaggerated. Embarrassing, really. If one of her films is shown locally, do go; just to see what I mean.'

Mildred paused. The room was breathless, stifling, even though she had troubled to unhook the curtains and roll up the blinds to the very top of the windows. Corbodéra's 'unexpectedly warm' weather was in reality torrid. Even the sea afforded no relief; it was blue molten glass, as warm as the air, so warm that bathing was almost pointless; it merely wet you and you felt more uncomfortable than before.

'*Author* Hunter is *supposed* to be working on another book, but those *three* machines of his must be rusting away. I do hear a peck or two now and then, but most of each day is spent ogling the great Gia. The artist, surprisingly, hasn't even turned his head. That's to his credit, I must say. And speaking of Eduard – *change of heart*! At least to a degree. I find he isn't half bad. He has lost some of his belligerence and become quite civil, not to say gallant. I played "postgirl" the other day, and when I delivered a letter to his room, he invited me in for my first glimpse of his work. I believe that is what changed my mind. The man is sincere! And he is working on a canvas . . . truly, it must be longer than thirty feet, and twice of me high! It is called "The Sea of Corbodéra". Unfortunately, he has been staggered (not "influenced") by Picasso, so there is more than a touch of *that* in it, but on the whole a kind of catholic eclecticism saves him. (Aren't I fancy today!) The painting – if categories are *ever* descriptive – is *ex*-pressionistic, *im*-pressionistic, *semi*-abstract – all of these; and none: his own. At first glance it seems non-objective, but in the very next instant you *do* begin to make things out, though it is *so* large that it is impossible to stand far enough away to see it *totum simul*; you are *in* the painting, so to speak, and begin to drown in a sea of colour. . . .'

Mildred sighed, lifting her pen from a fourth sheet of paper – all covered with her small even penmanship, so perfect it seemed almost printed.

It was exhausting: this 'bubbling' news, these endless pseudo-personal details about things that, even though they had actually happened in the way she described, were so coloured, so socially, conventionally stylised that they were the next best thing to a lie.

Eduard's room . . .

What *was* the truth? – if she could find it; and, if found, would she be able to bear it? Could she live in *that* sort of world? Wasn't the pseudo-personal a haven of sanity, a comforting ritual of pragmatic repose? Didn't it make life livable?

– Four flights of rickety, dark stairs, her heart pounding, not from the climb, but because *he* would open the door, and either slam it in her face or invite her in.

'– A letter for you, monsieur.' – The ridiculous, coy 'monsieur' because his father had been French.

Why had she troubled? Why had she waited almost two hours to waylay Señor Gutiérrez when he brought the mail, pretending to herself that she was looking for her own, never once admitting that a letter she could deliver to Eduard was what she'd wanted. – God! – it had been necessary to deliver *everyone*'s mail – even a postcard-advertisement for Nicky from a barber in Rome! And only, she finally knew, because a letter for Eduard was there among the rest.

'How thoughtful of you! – *mademoiselle*. But you should not have troubled.'

'– Oh, no trouble; no trouble at all.' – A kindness, a small benevolence. If he had knelt, she would have knighted him.

He *didn't* invite her in, but neither had he slammed the door. He merely stood there, letter in hand.

'Is there . . . something else?'

The truth now, the truth! Her laughter was gay but a bit tremulous.

'Forgive me . . . *Eduard*' – the first, no the second time she'd used his given name – 'but I am a woman, and I'm curious. The others have been talking so much . . . about your painting. . . .'

'Of *course.*'

The fascinating pig of a man had known she would come! – if not the pretext she would use. But what did it matter? She had what she wanted: the truth that was his room. Not its size or its magnificent view of the sea, not its pigsty artist's disorder (couldn't they ever work in a *tidy* room?) or even the shock of his painting – a fantastic colossus crucified on one wall. None of these. It was the small, the intimate details to which her eyes crowded: a half-finished peach into which his teeth had bitten, soiled underwear hanging on a hook behind a door, a frayed toothbrush in a glass by the sink, a bar of yellow soap which his hands had worn into the shape of a crude hour-glass, the dishevelled chintz-draped day-bed, darkened where he laid his head. . . .

3

ROBERT was 'writing' another of his novels. He was calling it 'Games for the Embryonic Child', and it concerned a certain Oliver Fartswell, a jaded, dissolute young socialite. '– A libertine,' he said, 'whose *raison d'être* was the extraordinary parties he gave. . . .'

'I have given *many* extraordinary parties,' Mrs Carter informed him. 'Not in recent years, of course; I no longer have the energy, the imagination required. . . .'

'Something unusual,' the novelist continued, 'always happened at these affairs. – At one party, for example, he arranged a most ingenious and humorous way to serve the wine. It seems he had an expert craftsman instal a small stone angel, a nude little boy, about three feet high, with wings, and so internalised with pumps and tubes that it was able to pee the wine in a constant stream. . . .'

'That *was* ingenious,' Mrs Carter conceded, quite caught up in the narrative.

Mildred was sitting firm and resolute, her shoulders tight, her needles flying. It was too humiliating, too tiresome to keep running off each time Robert opened his dirty mouth. But even as she sat, her resolution began to waver. There was something wildly shocking about Robert's story already; somehow the possibilities were horrendous.

The Countess was asleep in her beach chair, snoring gently; but Gia was an avid listener, along with Mrs Carter, and the Diers stopped their game of chess to watch the little drama before them.

'– To fill one's glass,' Robert went on, 'each guest had

merely to hold it under the charming and carefully chiselled little penis. . . .'

There was a faint airy sound; Mildred may have gasped, or coughed, but if she had done so it was drowned in the torrent of wild laughter that spewed from Gia's magnificent throat.

Robert waited. The laughter subsided, and Mildred remained. It was clear that at last she was determined to sit him out, a challenge he found stimulating. With a crinkle of his eyes in Paul Dier's direction, he continued:

'– Sadly, at the height of the festivities, the apparatus failed to function. It was due, apparently, to a small bubble in one of the tubes; consequently, the arc of wine began to fall and soon diminished to a few paltry drops. . . .'

The expression on Mrs Carter's face was almost tragic, so he hastened on to add that Mr Fartswell had been *warned* of this possibility and knew its remedy.

'After all,' Robert said, 'the apparatus was basically a syphon, and all that was needed to start it again . . .'

He had turned his head to speak directly to Mrs Carter, and when, barely seconds later, he looked back in Mildred's direction, her place was empty. Only her knitting remained, impaled on a solitary needle: a patch of blood-red wool in the sun.

4

HE thought he heard someone coming, and in mild panic lifted his head cautiously above the dune. It could have been Vicky; sometimes, if he was gone too long, she got that crazy loneliness of hers and wandered about the island – looking in the places where he usually played – calling his name in a creepy, far-away tone.

'Niiiiiii-cky' – like that, sad and peculiar. After his father died, his mother for a while had called him that way.

Oh now – his mother! – and his breath came quickly, answering the flood of swift-sweet pain that washed momentarily through his body.

It wasn't Vicky; it was only the *buedera*, who had learned to unlock her gate with her nose.

'Go home,' Nicky called; 'go home, *buedera*' – in a hoarse subdued shout, and the animal lifted her great moist eyes to his in a fixed stare.

Even the *buedera* likes to look at me, Nicky thought, for its round black eyes reminded him of Vicky's.

Last night he'd sat for more than an hour – the longest he'd ever sat since they'd come to the island – until he'd begun to sigh and fidget and pick boldly at his nose.

That always annoyed her; he could tell because she'd start twisting her rings or fingering the back of her neck as if she'd got a crick in it. It was a wonder she didn't have ten cricks. How could anyone look at something, anything, so long and not get tired? She sat as still as him; stiller; they were like two crazy statues; only he was allowed to move a little, though he tried not to: his head, or his hands; he could look at things, though there wasn't much ever to look at, he had looked at everything in her room so often.

'All right, all right, Nicky,' she'd said finally – which meant the sitting was over.

Nicky rolled to his stomach, almost crushing the tail end of his kite. Eduard had made it for him, out of some pink tissue paper he had in his room and the wires from an old umbrella. It flew pretty good when the wind was strong enough. Which it wasn't today. There'd been no wind at all since the heat had come to the island. Everyone sweated, and everyone drank all the time. No one could get enough water. Him too. Though heat never bothered him much. It used to get pretty hot in Brooklyn some summers. He remembered the street hydrants when the weather got too bad: the rust like blood for a while; then the cool-rushing stream and a million skinny white kids laughing and dancing. He'd had no bathing suit; he remembered that; his mother had sewn up the fly on one of his shorts. It was sort of embarrassing, having her sew them up and then looking at him careful-like after he'd put them on.

It came back again: the sick, pleasured ache for his mother. He felt so empty! Like there was no one in the whole world alive. Only him. And the blue, blue sky; the heat – flowing across the sand thick as water.

Vicky couldn't stand the heat, she kept cursing in her language, and three, maybe four times a day she sat in her rusty tub with the lion's claw feet and she'd send him for a bucket of ice cubes. 'Don't come in!' – her hand with all the big diamonds and jewels reaching out from behind the door for the bucket. She was funny! And always so sad. He loved her. He loved Vicky. When he'd been sick in Rome after his mother died. . . .

Oh his mother! Again and again. The ache, the crowding in his throat, like he could almost vomit. He *had* vomited in Rome. He thought it would never stop – coming up black and green – and then gagging and retching like there was something there but nothing coming up at all! Only air. He could have died. He would have – if it hadn't been for Vicky. She'd done everything, just like the doctor said, to bring down his fever. The alcohol – like ice on his body; two enemas, *two* – and as sick as he was he fought her off like a cat fights a dog. He remembered that: 'You get away!' – maybe he'd even cursed her and used dirty words – yelling and shouting until he was so weak he couldn't move. He remembered nothing after that, only when the world came back – and there she was, sitting by the wide, white bed with a bowl of cracked ice mixed with perfume, stroking his forehead with wet fingers. He loved Vicky! He would sit for a year if she wanted to look at him. For *two* years. Solid. And not move. Not even a finger. Sit still as dead.

'Niiiii-cky. . . .' *That*'s the way she called him! Like a flute, high-up. Sometimes it made him shiver.

He shivered now, despite the heat, because that flute-like high-up sound was in his head.

When the chill left him, he rolled on his back to feel the bite of the sun on his chest. It was a desert sun – misty – with a big ring around it – like the sun in movies about deserts when the people are dying of thirst and staggering up the dunes with their clothes in rags and their mouths cracked and covered with blisters.

Gia was in a movie about the desert. He'd heard her tell all about it, but she didn't die of thirst. She sang in a cabaret where the sheikhs came. Only that was just background. She was the wife of an oil engineer, and was raped

– so she said – by someone, maybe one of the sheikhs, and then went to sing in the cabaret.

Mrs Carter and Robert – everyone – begged her, so she sang the song from the picture for them. It was real good, but maybe kind of tuneless – like speaking more than singing, and her voice was so deep that if he didn't see the sounds coming out of her mouth he would have thought it was a man.

Gia laughed like a man, too; big and loud, from deep down in her throat. 'What did you find in your milk today?' – How she had tried not to laugh, then burst out like a volcano, almost spitting all over him, hugging him and whirling him around in a crazy dance. He had felt her body, like something humming with electricity, her warm, wide stomach pressed against his.

What a bathing suit she wore! In America she'd get arrested and hauled off to jail. It was like skin, and the colour of her skin.

How he would like to . . .

Mild, sweet, his boy's warm lust watered his mouth until he had to swallow. He felt the flood, the pleasured glow move to his heart, then gather in a growing heat in his belly.

Wow! he thought; wow! – the ache growing too vast to support, the reaching too insistent.

He turned to one side and dug a hole in the sand as deep as his trembling hand.

5

'No,' Robert said; 'it has to be perpendicular. We must be able to move, travel, *measure*, in a dimension not already established; that is, not *contained* in the other three.' He prodded at the skeletal image of the cube he had drawn in the sand. 'When we measure depth – here, we are measuring at right angles to length – here, and width – here.'

'I see,' Gia nodded.

'So, when we "measure" time – and a minute has no more reality than an inch – we are also measuring a dimension, but a new one, a new perpendicular. Clearly it is not contained in the other three, the spacial dimensions. And that is why we call it the "fourth" dimension.'

'I see,' Gia nodded.

Robert added: 'Here's another way of looking at it. Consider a line as an infinite repetition of a point. Then a square, or plane, is an infinite repetition of a line, and a cube – or any three-dimensional object – an infinite repetition of a plane, or two-dimensional object. Extending the analogy, what would the fourth dimension be?'

'Extending the *what*?' Gia inquired gently.

Robert laughed. 'The analogy. Now don't tell me you don't know the meaning of *that* word.'

'I'm sorry, signor.'

– Always 'signor'; sometimes 'my friend'. When would she begin to call him 'Robert'?

'Well the analogy . . .' Words of one syllable eluded him. He couldn't think. She was lying too close to him.

In her enthusiasm to hear every word, she had moved her body barely an inch from his, until every cell in him seemed agitated, turning and twisting like iron filings in the field of an uncertain magnet.

'It's a "for-instance",' he offered idiotically. '– And if a cube is an infinite repetition of a square, a four-dimensional body must be an infinite repetition of a cube.'

'I see,' Gia nodded.

'So there is a separate "you"'– he forced a smile –'for every second of your life. You are an infinite repetition of yourself.'

Gia's eyebrows raised themselves in lovely surprise.

'Does Mrs Carter know this?'

'Mrs Carter knows everything,' Robert answered. 'I have never mentioned a subject on which she couldn't elaborate for several hours.'

She was unbearably close. In a moment he would groan or shudder. He was becoming dizzy, and had the curious fantasy that his mind could snap and he'd pounce upon her like a savage, tearing at her flesh with his teeth. He shifted his position, separating their bodies by a good two feet.

To his embarrassment, she seemed to suspect the reason for his move.

'– But it remains an analogy,' he rushed on; 'it means nothing, or everything. It is a way of acquiring esoteric knowledge: intuitions, insights that the mind can't grasp, can't "think" at all.'

– So he seduced her. – With a syllogism. He ached to lean forward and take her in his arms; his throat and chest were pained and tight with longing to put his mouth to hers.

He hadn't the strength, the will to even touch her fingers.

She climbed stairs, walked miles, crossed countless roads – even stumbled down the stony ravine beside the church ruin to look hopefully at the *valdepeñas* – without the comfort – the courtesy – of a hand on her elbow.

6

IF he didn't come to the beach with the others, she found herself waiting expectantly, and waiting, God yes, impatiently. If, after hours, he didn't appear at all, her disappointment was undeniable, as real as her heart-beat – such a flood of angry sensations in her body that her irritable hands began to drop stitches.

If he did appear, though they barely spoke, smiling with deliberate politeness at each other – she spent all her time watching him, listening avidly if he spoke to the others or – though so rarely – if he addressed himself to her.

If he swam, if he walked, if he merely shifted his body on the sand, her eyes were there instantly, following every move. And if she did not watch him directly, if there was no possible excuse to lift her eyes and stare at him frankly – when he played ball with Nicky for example – she made sure he was well within her periphery vision. She stared at the sea, but looked at Eduard. She knitted or talked – with increasing gaiety and animation she noticed! – and looked at Eduard. She reclined in a beach chair, sleeping! – but her eyes were open the barest, imperceptible slit, and there he was: Eduard: crowding her vision.

His fishnet bathing suit had rotted and fallen apart – she had heard him joking about it with Marion – so now he wore his cut-off dungarees. They were equally affected – with their big smear of vermilion and splatter of green – but certainly more modest, and for that she should have been grateful.

– *Should have been!*

Lying sleepless, fevered in her bed thinking these thoughts, Mildred was sick with shame.

Most unbearable and shocking of all: she noticed that she carefully positioned herself on the sand when Eduard came to the beach. There always seemed an exact place, a precise spot she must sit in, in relation to him. Why anything so – *silly*? – so, yes, *humorous* in a way. Such foolishness!

It was not humorous, or silly, or foolish. The reason for it was the most shameful, the most disgusting discovery of her life. *She was sitting downwind*! Yes! She always placed Eduard between the wind and herself so she could *smell* that generally unwashed pig of a man – that subtle, musky-maled, turpentined odour that was as exciting to her, she now knew, as the smell of baking bread to the hungry.

This rude, crude man! Not man at all! – *animal*. What did she hope for, what did she want?

God, dear God. . . . How it forced itself upon her, how the breath-soft dream 'happened'. It was always *there*, in the past moment, already 'existing', and in the present moment she half-allowed herself to capture it.

Eduard: his firm, brown body. Eduard: the lean, smooth-muscled length, breadth, areas of his maleness. Eduard: the marvellous line of black hair that ran from his chest to his navel, spreading, widening into a dense curled tip of a triangle above the rusted belt of his ragged dungarees.

Eduard . . .

7

'NOT only that,' Paul went on, 'but I once met an analyst who didn't believe in the unconscious at all. Truly. He said there was no such thing; it simply didn't exist. – So you are in good company.'

'Did I say I didn't *believe* in it?' Robert asked, rather peevishly. 'I *said* – that it is difficult for me to believe a dichotomy exists in *myself*, separating consciousness from my so-called "unconscious" self.'

'I'm not sure the unconscious can be described as a "self",' Paul returned. 'It has no discoverable "centre", so to speak. At least . . .'

'Well – "contents" then,' Robert interrupted. 'Obviously it is composed of *something*: drives, impulses, wishes, fears, desires – all of them so antithetic to the conscious "image" of oneself – isn't that it? – that all kinds of ruses and disguises are employed to express them. I don't quarrel with that; one has to be blind not to observe it with merciless regularity, but I maintain that the ruses, the disguises, are increasingly outmoded – obsolete.'

Paul smiled and inclined his head. He enjoyed talking with Robert, but talking with Robert usually meant arguing with him – and while arguing with him, trying to decide at what point the man was serious and at what point he was not. '– Do you dream?' he asked.

'Constantly,' Robert returned. 'And my dreams support my contention. Every symbol is so transparent to me that I wonder why my unconscious doesn't tire of its mumbo-jumbo. Since it can deceive no one of the slightest intelligence and sensitivity, least of all myself, why does it persist in its idiotic assumption that its language is esoteric? If anything, in our day and age, the unconscious is vestigial; it is like a woman who insists on dressing herself up in mysterious veils when we have already seen her lying naked before us a thousand times.'

Paul's smile deepened. He shook his head briefly. 'The unconscious is – by its very definition' – he threw up his hands – 'unconscious. What you are saying . . .'

Again Robert interrupted.

'I dream of a shoe,' he said; 'an uncomfortable shoe; a shoe with a nail in it. What could be more insulting? I die of shame that my unconscious should express itself quite so naïvely. A child would know the meaning of a nail in a shoe.'

'The child in you dreamed the dream,' Paul said.

Robert was visibly piqued. '– I'm simply illustrating. I'm not reporting an actual dream.'

'– Merely a fantasy.'

'I would hardly distinguish it to that extent.' – God, the man could be irritating! And he looked so cool, so damnably cool in this infernal heat, relaxing comfortably in his chair, sipping his drink, his legs crossed on the balustrade. ' – I chose arbitrarily – at random.'

'– Like putting your hand in a grab bag,' Paul returned. 'One never knows *what* will happen.' Did he imagine it, or was Robert actually angry? He went on rapidly, almost without a pause: '– You see how generous I am. The grab bag was *my* fantasy. – Because I am your friend, not your analyst.'

Robert was disarmed, and silent. He stared toward the sea, adding presently: 'I find it increasingly difficult to talk and make sense.' He sighed, his voice softened and slow, devoid of its usual brisk quality. 'Sometimes I think that Freud has ruined everything.'

Paul uncrossed his legs promptly; his spine straightened itself of its own accord. But the writer went on: '– He has added another dimension to language and thought, so complex that we are all staggering like drunkards in an unmanageable space. Do you know – I occasionally write a paper, even give a semester of lectures as if he never existed – for the sheer luxury of simplicity, and despite its dishonesty. Last year, I gave an entire survey course in English literature and barely mentioned his name.' He laughed suddenly. 'One of my students, I recall, was very upset about the "Ancient Mariner". What did the Albatross *represent* psychoanalytically; why had Coleridge chosen a *dead bird*? And wasn't there, possibly, some *oedipal* significance to Coleridge's preoccupation with water and snakes? – I couldn't shut him up; every time I turned from the blackboard his hand was flying. I found it convenient to lose my temper finally, and remind him that I was teaching English Literature, not Abnormal Psyche. His reply – listen to this – was that the real value and pleasure of literature consisted of the author's revelations of himself in and through his work. A college freshman! That wasn't all! The most significant thing about Kafka, I was informed, was his father – and the fascination of Shakespeare's sonnets the fact that they were written for and to a man! And what, he inquired, was interesting about *Paradise Lost*, one of the dreariest poems in the English language? Before I could reply, he answered his own question with one word. "Milton," he said – and dropped my course.'

Paul nodded. 'Literature isn't like maths,' he said, 'or the languages, or any of the sciences. Even psychology gets on beautifully without Freud. Abnormal Psychology *teaches* him, of course – either well or badly. . . .'

'That *is* the point there,' Robert agreed. 'His principles are the subject of the inquiry, not the object to which his principles might be applied.'

'So the English Department suffers!' Paul concluded.

'But pretends not to,' Robert replied. 'Most of my colleagues admit no problems at all. They drag in Freud by the hair, and throw him out quite as rudely. Nor will they admit that the great task of literature, if it is to survive as literature, is to absorb Freud. – Of necessity, our contemporary writers have had to meet the man head on, but what has happened? – with pathetically few exceptions – Joyce was one – they have nodded sagely – presumably in agreement – and gone on writing as if he never existed. Others who were shattered by the collision are turning out books that are little more than clinical case histories.' He paused. 'In the end, art has always ingested science; it has been a boa constrictor, slowly squeezing the life from it and swallowing it whole. But today, literature has not even begun to unhinge its jaws; it has been too staggered by its prey. . . .'

The analogy was inaccurate and extravagant, but there it was. And Paul seemed impressed. Or perhaps merely kind. Robert rose, pacing as he always paced at a lecture's end, searching for a final light touch, the unrelated *bon mot* that was like the snap of his fingers, un-hypnotising his students, returning them to a world of mundane sense and sensibility in a cheerful frame of mind. He dug his hands deep into his pockets, lifting his eyes to the sea. And there it was: his light touch; his unrelated *bon mot*. Nicky was playing by the water's edge, his faded red polo shirt a violet blur in Corbodéra's intense blue twilight.

'Ah, Nicky!' he said with a tremulous sigh. 'Ah, that boy!' – and Paul, following his gaze, began to laugh.

8

'. . . BUT what are we going to *do* with the unconscious?'
Mrs Carter inquired with a helpless look at the others. 'No
one has said *that.*'

The Countess winked at Nicky. 'I think we ought to
give it back to the Indians' – and then she guffawed in her
ribald way.

'Victoria is never serious,' Mrs Carter complained to the
Diers.

'– Because you are all so foolish,' the Countess replied.
'Someone mentioned Buchenwald – as if it were a summer
day-camp! – What is the unconscious going to do with *us*?
That is the question. I watch. I am eternally on guard.
Because it is a stealthy animal – and it pounces!' She made
sudden claws at Nicky who jerked his head back in alarm.
'No, no, my plum.' She stroked his cheek. 'It will not
pounce on you – only on the others. – Because they are
stupid.'

'To hear you,' Marion said, 'one would think it was all
bad.'

'Could it be worse?'

Victoria jabbed the air with jewelled hands. 'What is
history but a record of its seizures – one convulsion after
another – when nations foam at the mouth and tear at
each other like dogs.' She was being very dramatic and Mrs
Carter thought she might as well sit back and enjoy it.

'Only the individual is mad,' Paul said. 'To speak of
national madness . . .'

'I hit you with one bean,' Victoria interrupted, 'and

121

you do not even feel it; if I put a thousand beans in a bag and clobber you over the head your brains are gone.'

'But I agree,' Paul said; 'I merely wished to point out . . .'

'I was there, in Germany before the war,' Victoria went on. 'And it was almost tangible – this madness. It lived in the streets and in the air; you saw it in people's eyes, burning like a fever. You could not live with it, even near it without becoming infected. And I was as infected as the rest in the beginning. Never have I had such gooseflesh!' She laughed. 'That was the Führer's secret, you know. "– Give the people gooseflesh; with gooseflesh they will do anything," he said to me.'

'You knew Hitler?' Suzette inquired.

'No one *knew* him,' Victoria replied. 'I was with him for a bit when the fever was a rosy glow on his cheek. Once I slept with him.' She smiled, glancing at Nicky. '– Don't look so shocked, my grape. I am being literal. We had spent a whole day mountain-climbing at Berchtesgaden hunting for wild flowers and were very tired. So we lay down in a meadow and slept.'

'What kind of a man was he?' Gia inquired.

'Gentle,' Victoria replied, '– sweet; a darling moustached little boy – you could not resist brushing the lock of hair from his forehead; that is what it was there for, of course, but also a hungry baby – with sharpened teeth – ready to drink your blood if he got near your jugular vein. – I will tell you a secret. He had a doll. "*Mein Liebchen*" he called her – with yellow braided hair and round blue eyes. He kept her since he was a baby. "– For one of the village children," he insisted.' She grabbed Nicky in a wild laughing bear hug. '– That village child must have grey hair – and not even the diaper from *Mein Liebchen*'s fat behind.'

She released the boy, commanding: 'Stand up; show

them the weight you have gained on Corbodéra. Show them your muscle – the left one; it is bigger than the other.'

Nicky stood up.

'See!' Victoria cried, kneading the calves of his legs. 'Flesh! Flesh on those bones! – Soon he will be fat enough to eat. – An apple in the mouth, and into the oven he goes! Now your muscle. Come now, don't be shy. Show them.'

Nicky bent one of his frail arms, making a fist, straining his shoulders and neck until his face was rosy pink, and truly, a tiny round bulge appeared. Marion was amazed.

'Like Tarzan,' she said.

'Who?' the Countess inquired.

'Tar-zan. He is an American ape-man, a forest creature of great physical beauty and prowess.'

'Ah – I should like to meet him.'

Marion laughed. 'Well, I'm afraid you can't. He is a literary creation.'

'They have made movies about him,' Gia said.

'– But about the unconscious,' Mrs Carter insisted. 'If only Robert were here! And Mildred! – she has become a veritable recluse. – Paul, you haven't said a word, and you are the one who should truly know best. – About the unconscious I mean. Of course, I always *knew* it was naughty; but I also thought it was the source of inspiration: of poetry, music, literature. . . . It seems to me that artists are always "tapping" their unconscious. The early poets used to call it the "Muse"– none of them could write at all, it seemed, without first "invoking" the Muse. It was always "Hail to thee . . ." or "Come, blithe spirit . . ." – some such thing. They were always – *helpless*, waiting for the Muse to come up from the depths to take care of things. And *I* believe that she was simply the unconscious – or part of it, if it does have parts.' She thought for a moment.

123

'– I do believe it must. Can you name anything, anything at all that doesn't have parts? – Remember the molecule? They thought they had got to the very bottom of things – the indivisible unit out of which every material thing was composed. But along came the atom – and positive and negative electrons, and anti-matter, and now even the nuclei have nuclei. I believe that is the latest thing. – So the Muse may simply have been part of the unconscious; she lived "down there", so to speak. But it must have been lonely. No one bothered to call her up after a while. There were no more "Come, blithe spirits . . ." Not a single one.' Mrs Carter laughed suddenly. '– So she moved to Hollywood. Or is about to.' And she stared at Gia with a happy expression.

'I am having a swimming pool,' the actress exclaimed. 'It plays music. You will come to visit me. All of you.' She sat up on the sand, quite excited. 'I am having twenty-two rooms – so there is space for everyone, even if my brothers and sisters are there. You will visit? Next year, perhaps? In the spring?'

Everyone promised, including the Diers who looked at each other questioningly before nodding their heads.

'How big is the pool?' Nicky asked.

Gia shrugged. 'Well – it is big; tremendous. A block long; two.'

The boy's eyes widened.

'– Now about the unconscious. . . .' Mrs Carter said.

9

'. . . THE hands of the clock are usually pointing to six-forty-five, though sometimes it is nine-thirty. And I am late – hours late; I feel dismayed, frantic. I have the almost-sense of the nightmare – of tremendous – *pressures, dislocations*. I try to dress, but I have trouble getting into my clothes. Nothing fits.' She smiled, but with a touch of wonder and fright. '– Everything is too large, or too small – not mine at all, as if it belonged to a dwarf, or a giant! I struggle – and finally manage to get something on. I look at myself in the mirror, and I'm a *mess*: a clown, a caricature of myself. My lipstick is a wild smear; I've put on a frightful amount of rouge. I look like . . . a street-walker; truly – just *awful!* '

It was Mildred's dream; according to her a recurrent one.

– Wonderfully rich and interesting – but weren't all dreams rich and interesting? – or most of them. Paul had enjoyed every minute of its telling – and every gesture, every pause, every word-emphasis Mildred had given it. His mind teemed with instant possibilities – and for the first time on Corbodéra, the first time since his marriage, really, he was impatient to get back to work.

But now that Mildred had told him her dream, and sat at the table before him sipping coffee, what was there to say? She, and Marion – all of them – attributed to him knowledge, insight, ability no one could possibly possess.

'What is the meaning of a *bird*?' Marion would ask. Or, 'If I dream of a knife and cutting my finger, but no blood appears – what does *that* mean; what is the meaning of no blood?'

Victoria was impossible. Her dreams were elaborate pageants, Technicolor extravaganzas 'with a cast of thousands', usually with an exotic Greek, Roman or Egyptian background, though once she had dreamed of a 'bank in Brooklyn' where she had blasted a hole in a wall to gain access to the money. The dominant theme portrayed catacombs, tombs, crypts, vaults which she ransacked of treasure: jewels, gold, exquisite statuary, priceless art.

And now Mildred: the shyest of them all, the one who had not so far discussed her dreams with him: here she was with her clocks and streetwalker outfit, late for one of the most important appointments of her unconscious life. . . .

He had to say to her what he had been saying to the others with monotonous regularity, and to which no one paid the slightest heed.

'Mildred: there are very few dream symbols which we can with any certainty label "universal" – that is, to which any absolute universality of interpretation can be applied. A few approach it, perhaps – the snake dreams, the dreams of flying, or falling, of being stabbed, or strangled. . . . But two people, or a dozen people, may employ the same symbol – and in each case the deepest level of meaning when it is finally uncovered may be entirely different.'

She was so clearly disappointed that he could not leave it there. 'But it is a rich dream,' he went on; '– the clocks, the dreaming of being asleep and waking up *in* the dream – that is particularly interesting. I'm sure it would prove a rewarding dream were you in analysis and had an opportunity to free-association. I take it – you have never been in analysis.'

Mildred shook her head. 'I don't believe in it,' she replied firmly, and in the next moment was acutely embarrassed. '– What a dreadful thing to say! I'm sorry. It's rather like *your* telling me that you don't believe in education – in teaching children.'

Paul smiled. 'Well – there are differences.'

'Certainly I believe in psychiatric care,' Mildred amended. 'We cannot – simply *abandon* our mentally ill, can we?'

'We cannot,' Paul agreed.

'– But to spend years on an analyst's couch . . .'

'The thought appals you.'

Mildred hesitated, then nodded. 'Frankly, yes.' She patterned the tablecloth with her fork, adding: 'The technique, the *method* appals me. – Simply to talk – to say anything that comes into one's head in the hope of reviving . . . repressed memories? Isn't that it? – Forbidden desires, urges . . .'

'That's part of it,' Paul replied. He paused. '– You don't believe such things exist. You don't believe in the unconscious?' ·

The direct question troubled Mildred. She thought about it carefully and answered: 'I don't know. I simply don't know.'

'Fortunately, the unconscious believes in *you*,' Paul offered as a joke.

Mildred didn't smile. 'How is that?' she asked.

'– It seems to have taken good care of you all your life. It makes you sleep when you're tired and wakes you refreshed. It digests your food and pumps blood through your veins and grows your – very attractive – hair.'

This time Mildred did smile. 'I don't mean *that*,' she said, pouring more coffee for both of them. 'You're joking.'

'– But quite serious,' Paul returned, refusing the cream.

'Is the body a machine? – Or a chemical factory? Why take all this magnificent and incredibly complicated work for granted? *Something* is there – "doing" it all – and it seldom complains. – Though I do hear you have ear trouble and are subject to sea-sickness. – Surely you're not going to claim credit for all this astonishing labour!'

'No,' Mildred laughed; 'I'm afraid I can't. I can't claim credit for growing my hair.'

'Then won't you admit that you believe in one form of unconscious life? And if you admit that, you must admit the possibility of others.' Dared he? – Suzette wasn't here to stop him. 'Mildred – what dressed you up in a street-walker's outfit – what rouged your cheeks and pointed the hands of the clock to half-past nine?'

'But——' Mildred stammered, her laughter subsiding; 'it's so . . . *completely* opposed to my nature, so . . . *ridiculous*.'

'You're calling it what Freud called it,' Paul observed; '– it: *id*. – And I do not agree that it's "opposed" to your nature; the small part of you that you've decided to *call* your "nature" is opposed to "*it*".'

'I'm not sure I understand. . . .' Mildred's brow was wrinkled, her lips pursed.

'Every woman is a latent streetwalker,' he said bluntly; 'It's part of being a woman.'

She took it well – *bravely* was the word; probably because simply not believing it helped. It was too 'opposed' to her nature. And Paul was just a bit ashamed. He was becoming as much a tease as Robert Hunter – and enjoying himself.

'But that is neither here nor there in relation to your dream,' he went on, more gently. 'I see that I am doing exactly what I said couldn't be done: I am labelling it "universal". Mildred – I don't know *what* your dream

128

means. I couldn't possibly know. I have as much right to interpret it as . . . Nicky Passanante. The dream is an elaborate structure, intricate architecture . . . exquisitely composed. Were you my patient, you might talk for hours, days . . . and not even begin to exhaust the material it contains. You would associate to every element in it . . . the clocks, for example, the dream-time . . . why six-forty-five or half-past nine? – in each case a six and a nine. . . .'

He stopped abruptly, the expression on his face that of a man who has said something he hadn't intended to say. But he had said nothing that made sense to her; merely: 'Why six-forty-five or half-past nine? – in each case a six and a nine. . . .' She could think of nothing in her life, past or present, that involved a six and a nine. Then suddenly it struck her.

'I was born June ninth,' she said excitedly; 'on the ninth day of June. – Do you see?'

Paul didn't momentarily.

'June is the sixth month,' she went on; 'I was born on the ninth day of the sixth month!'

'It's a birth dream,' Paul said, looking peculiarly relieved. 'It refers to your birth, or the conditions of your birth. Or perhaps——' to be done with it, he put on his turban '– perhaps to *re*-birth. Perhaps it indicates that something *new* will happen to you; some – inner development, an important – insight; perhaps a widening, an expansion of the personality, a growth in understanding. . . .'

Mildred was very pleased with her fortune.

'It's *fascinating*,' she said. 'Perhaps there is something to this dream symbolism after all.'

10

'He is truly talented,' Victoria said, 'but looking at it, I felt like an ant on an elephant's knee.'

Nicky laughed.

'I make him mad. I keep asking what it means. – But he never tells me.'

'I don't wonder,' Victoria returned. 'That is a stupid question.' She was making up her eyes before her mirror, and was today applying black instead of green. 'It is a painting. That's what it means.'

'– But all those colours, and mixed-up shapes! I don't know *what* they are!'

'They are exactly that – colours and mixed-up shapes.' She turned, brush in hand, one eye so dark it was like the fake telescopes you look through that give you a black eye.

'– But it's supposed to be the ocean. It's called "The Sea of Corbodéra".'

'The painting is an "abstract",' Victoria returned. '– or a semi-abstract, if it must have a name. Which means' – she smiled a little – 'that the artist *abstracts* – that is, *takes out, selects, portrays, shows* – what he considers to be the essence——' she hesitated '– the particular *character* or *spirit* of the subject . . . which he interprets freely – in whatever shapes, forms and colours seem to him emotionally appropriate – descriptive of his *inner* experience.'

Nicky nodded wisely.

'I know,' he said.

But presently – 'All those crazy colours! – And boats that are just – *triangles*! They're even lopsided.'

Victoria returned to her eyes, spitting on her brush.

'So?' she inquired.

'He *says* they're boats.'

'– Then they must be. What else could they be?' She sighed a little. '– How many times have I seen you take a bit of wood or folded paper and float it on the water?'

Nicky frowned. 'That's different.'

'I think not. What is the difference between a bit of wood or folded paper and a painted triangle? And tell me this: how often have you seen Corbodéra's sunset – the wonderful clouds and colours: blue, pink, violet, green: each day different, each time new and exciting?'

'– Many times. Every night.'

'And do you ask what it *means*?'

Nicky sucked at his bottom lip, thinking.

'– No.'

'Then why must you ask so stupidly what the artist's painting *means*? What do all those colours and shapes in the sky *mean*?'

'Well——' Nicky dried his mouth. '– They mean that the sun is setting I guess.'

Victoria threw up her hands.

'You are getting too old,' she complained, 'and already twisted in your thinking. You must start growing young.' She turned to him, both eyes black. '– I will give you a lesson. What does the rain mean? – When it rains?'

Nicky thought carefully.

'– It means that water is coming from the sky. It means that things are getting wet.'

'Oh!——'

Victoria suffered. '– You are impossible. "Getting wet!" When you pee on a flower it is getting wet too. I suppose it is raining.'

'Well——' he replied, trying to suppose he *did* pee on

131

flowers, which he didn't, 'yes – in a way. In that case, I am raining on the flower.'

Vicky's eyebrows rose.

'Ah,' she said. 'That is not bad. Perhaps you will be saved after all. Your corruption is superficial.'

No one spoke English. No one said anything that made any sense.

'Well, what *does* the rain mean?' Nicky demanded.

'It doesn't *mean* anything,' Victoria replied, her eyes beginning to reach outward. They always seemed hungry, as if they were mouths instead of eyes, ready to take things in and chew them up. 'What is the meaning of two plus two? – And don't tell me four. It means nothing – unless you happen to be adding apples, or counting the number of times you have gone to the bathroom today. What is the meaning of the moon? What does the sea mean? Rain is rain: it is a sound in the head, a touch on the skin. To say that it *means* this or that, is to add to the confusion. You'll never get out. You'll be stuck for the rest of your life.'

'Where?' Nicky asked. 'Where will I be stuck?'

'– Wherever you are, of course.'

'But I am here – on Corbodéra!'

'*Are* you, Nicky?' Victoria wondered darkly. 'Aren't you more often in America – and sometimes in Rome? I call you and my voice must travel to Brooklyn. I am getting hoarse.'

And she crossed the room and threw herself on the gold settee, reminding Nicky, as she so often did, of the movie actresses they had in olden times – the way they clenched their fist against their heart or right in the centre of their forehead. There was even the black around her eyes, and today she had wound a string of pearls through her hair.

'Brooklyn,' she repeated, and sat up. 'It has a pleasant

sound. *Are* there brooks there; is that why it is called that? Are things green, and wet, and young?'

Nicky didn't reply. He couldn't. He lowered his head, watching his fingers pick at each other.

'So!' Victoria said, rising. 'We pick at our fingers while the shadows lengthen, and comets appear in the sky.' She crossed to the window, pulling aside the blue gauze curtains to stare at the sea.

'There are buildings there,' Nicky said, straining for words that would be adequate, 'sort of very old buildings where I lived. All falling apart. With roaches. We had roaches, though we killed them all the time. It's a big place; I *told* you; and I couldn't tell you how different different parts are. Some parts are like the country – with trees. Maybe there *are* brooks, though I never did see one. But, like I said, we lived in a beat-up old building, a tenement I guess . . . in a section called Flatbush.'

'Flat Bush,' Victoria repeated, turning. 'That is an ugly name.'

Nicky shrugged. 'I suppose. I never thought about it much.'

'Well, think about it now. Get it done, finished, settled. We must learn to be where we are, and not be drowned in all the things we never thought about.'

Nicky thought about it. 'All right,' he said. 'It *is* ugly.' He frowned. '– What are we doing this for?'

Victoria opened both hands, palms to the sky. '– We don't have to. – It is too hot for the beach. – Go to the artist's room. Or play your radio. What is the game for today?'

Nicky's face brightened. 'It's the Yankees versus the White Sox.'

'Ah. Then go – listen. I must do my nails; but when Micky Mantle goes to bat, you must call me.'

133

She held his face in her hands, gazing at it as she would have gazed at the Holy Grail – with a tenderness that brought a lump to his throat and made him swallow. Then she smoothed his hair, and kissed his angel's forehead.

For a moment Eduard wasn't sure it *was* Mildred. Her face was as brightly, crudely painted as a harlot's, and she wore a filmy white négligé which she held caught up from the floor in a twisted, tight knot beneath her breasts. She appeared to have cut her own hair; it was chopped off and wild, arranged across her clown-white forehead in ringlets of ridiculous curls. Her feet, he noticed, were bare.

How she dared to walk through the hotel corridors in this unbelievable get-up, even at two in the morning, was unimaginable. The most idiotic of explanations occurred to him: she was inviting him to an impromptu masquerade; she was winning a bet – someone had dared her. . . . But then he saw the letter.

She shook so violently as she offered it to him that the envelope fluttered to the floor, and as they bent simultaneously to pick it up, Eduard's face bumped against the top of Mildred's head.

'Oh, my God!' she said.

'It's quite all right,' Eduard replied, holding his nose. The blow had been so sharp and painful that his eyes began to water. 'I see you have *another* letter for me, mademoiselle.'

The girl didn't answer, merely offering him the note with one hand while the other clung to the door jamb, supporting a body so weak it seemed on the verge of collapse.

He took the envelope with a nod of bewildered and

dubious appreciation, preparing to close the door. But there she stood, waiting.

The envelope, unsealed, was addressed 'For Eduard', and a large ink-spot in one corner had been partially erased.

What could he do? He removed the letter, unfolding the heavy white notepaper.

In letters an inch tall, as crudely penned as if a child had written it, were three words: 'I love you.'

Eduard stared at the message until the silence became an ache. He then cleared his throat and braced himself for a glance at the girl.

'Thank you, mademoiselle. It is kind of you.'

The tension drained from Mildred's body. She smiled, her teeth startlingly white against the vermilion smear of her mouth, and gasped greedily at the air.

'It's done!' she cried hoarsely. 'Now you know. You know!' and she moved boldly into the room, leaning over the back of a chair in staggered relief.

Eduard hesitated, thinking it best to leave the door open, but the sight of the girl in her nightgown, mascara'd tears of relief streaked down her cheeks, prompted him to shut it.

It was a mistake.

'Eduard!' she murmured. And with breathless passion: 'Oh, Eduard!' Her extended hands began to caress the air between them. 'It was so difficult, so very difficult. – To sacrifice – everything! If only you knew the pain, the anguish! I wrote a *thousand* notes . . . and tore them up. I thought of *ten* thousand ways to come to you, to let you know . . .'

'Yes,' Eduard said, fidgeting; 'but——'

'– And it was all so foolish. Because it is so *easy*. Simply to tell the truth . . . to say to someone, "I love you. . . ."'

'Mademoiselle – Do you think it wise? – That is, per-haps you ought not – I mean——'

'No one saw me. Truly. I was very careful. The lobby is deserted. No one knows. No one could guess.'

'I don't mean that. What I mean——'

'Yes?' She waited, watching Eduard shift uncomfort-ably from one foot to the other. He pulled at his beard, sniffed audibly, as if he had a cold.

A touch of Mildred's anxiety returned; her hand moved beneath one breast, feeling the sudden erratic beat of her heart.

'Eduard——' –Softly; with a nuance of surprise. '– Don't you *understand*? I'm offering you . . . my *all*.'

Eduard stared at her – her painted face and chopped hair and thin négligé – with a mixture of disbelief and distress, tempted strongly to be cruel, stayed by the warmth of pity. If her attitude hadn't been quite so martyred, if there had been even a suggestion of humour, of fun – even of deliberate wickedness in her – his pity might have won.

He crossed to a chair, sitting on the arm.

'And what might that be, mademoiselle?' he asked softly.

Mildred swallowed, one hand beginning to pick at the other.

'What might what be?' she asked, confused.

'– Your "all".' He paused. '– Since you come empty-handed, aside from your absurd and childish note – and in the sheerest of négligés, I take it that your "all" is a particular part of your anatomy.'

Mildred's face turned grey under the paint.

'I . . .' she said.

'Come now,' Eduard continued. 'Where is this jewel? – This priceless "all" that you have brought me?'

Mildred grew roots into the floor beneath her. She was as still, as lifeless, as a winter landscape.

'Come, come, mademoiselle. Let us not dilly-dally. Lift up your skirt; I've a suspicion that your "all" is between your legs, and I am curious to see this treasure.'

In the silence that followed, Eduard crossed the room, his back to her. He picked up a brush from a jar of turpentine, fingering the wet end of it. He turned, rubbing his hands dry.

'For two months, mademoiselle,' he said calmly, 'you have taken pains to make yourself unattractive to me. You have challenged the most cherished of my beliefs, violently criticised my opinions and my taste, ridiculed my wearing apparel, and, what is unforgivable, openly questioned my artistic integrity. And now——' he paused, letting his eyes linger on her figure, 'now you come to me at two in the morning with paint on your face and this – *cheesecloth* draped around you.'

Mildred found a voice; not her own, but at least one that could make intelligible sounds.

'*It is silk,*' she hissed; '*the sheerest of silk.*'

'– From your hope chest no doubt.'

She began to shake with impotent fury.

'You pig,' she said; 'you pig of a man!'

'Now, now.'

'– After you did everything in your power to attract me. – Parading yourself and that crude body of yours like a flag on a pole!'

'*I* did that, mademoiselle? – Surely you need glasses. You have been knitting too much, I'm afraid. The truth is, you have deceived yourself. I know you – only too well. You are like a great number of pathetic women who all their lives despise sex, revile men. Given an axe and the freedom to use a few of your suppressed criminal instincts,

138

I dare say you would have taken pleasure in chopping off those parts of me which now, suddenly, actualise your desire.'

'*You* . . . son of a bitch,' Mildred breathed, possessed. 'You obscene pig of a half-dressed savage. Given an axe, I would *gladly* chop it off – every inch, right down to its rotten poisonous root!'

He hadn't expected quite that. And watching her struggle for air, her hands kneading and clawing insanely at each other, Eduard was instantly frightened, and regretted all he had said.

'Mademoiselle,' he said gently, 'you are taking yourself and me and the situation too seriously. Sometimes I play a game with words. But truly, I know what it must have cost you – to come to me like this, and believe me, despite everything, I am flattered, and grateful.'

He put a hand to her shoulder reassuringly, and at his touch, Mildred, a sudden doll sewn of cloth and sawdust, was limp and dangling in his arms.

'Take me,' she murmured, her phthalo-green eyelids flickering, 'Eduard, take me; you must!' and in the next moment she was unconscious, her painted doll's head crazily bobbing and awry, as if the wire that fastened it to the shoulders had suddenly snapped.

'Good God!' Eduard said, and awkwardly dragged her to a chair.

He had covered her forehead and cheeks with turpentine before he realised it wasn't water.

Cursing, his hands trembling, he filled a pan and emptied it over her head, saturating her négligé. The silk became transparent, clinging so wetly to her breasts and torso that she appeared quite naked.

'Good God!' he repeated, slapping her cheeks, rubbing her hands.

Her dreamy eyes fluttered open.

'Are you all right?'

She glanced about dazedly, taking some moments to recover.

'Yes,' she said finally. 'Yes, I think so.'

That was all he needed. He dragged her gently but strongly to her feet, guiding her across the room.

'You must go now,' he said firmly, opening the door. 'Tomorrow everything will seem better. Everything will be fine. Tomorrow.'

'Tomorrow,' Mildred repeated, stupefied.

He had the courtesy or the idiocy to say, 'Good night', and with it, closed the door quickly behind her.

The lock clicked, and in the darkened corridor, Mildred gathered the wet, gossamer-thin silk of her négligé together to cover her all, and stood for a moment paralysed, reeking of turpentine, drained of life, every inch of her body a holocaust of shame.

Part Four

I

To the north of Cove Minor where Corbodéra narrowed to a thread, then widened into a crude white fist of jutting chalkland, a ragged fissure cracked through the cliffs at dawn. Like a giant arrow – almost silently except for an eerie hiss of sound – a wedge of chalk thousands of tons in weight plunged into the waiting sea. In its wake, the water cascaded in a bursting flower of pale green fire, then churned and boiled under a ghostly cloud of powdered chalk and mist.

The only one there to appreciate this awesome display was Pablo Gonzales – Corbodéra's old and mangy crow who leaped from his night perch as if one of his few fine tail feathers had been ruthlessly plucked from his behind.

Pablo had grown a cataract over one eye, but the left one was still good, and it was this he turned on the shattered land below, seeing what he saw.

'Caw!' he said; 'caw!' – which was the only word he knew.

2

'ART,' Eduard said thickly, his eyes narrowed and blood-shot, 'is today attempting to emulate music, just as poetry once tried to, and the result is a fiasco, too – a meaningless hodge-podge of pretty shapes and colours. – No, my friend: art that loses its human quality, its human meaning – loses its supreme human value. That is the truth of Picasso. He had the wisdom, or the instinct, perhaps, to resist the atrophy of non-objectivity.'

Robert shrugged. He was becoming bored and impatient, anxious to leave the studio. – Even a bit nervous. There was a growing wildness in Eduard, a lack of control; he'd had much too much to drink.

'These others,' the artist went on; 'they are art's delinquents: not children, understand, with the innocence and freshness of children, but babies – infants expressing anarchy at its source, in its purest form. Pollock, for your information, had unrelieved dysentery: he dribbled a forest of shit on his canvases.'

Robert rose – and was pushed rudely back into his chair.

'– Which is not to suggest,' Eduard went on, his drunken splendour increasing, 'that all art – painting that is, isn't fæcal in origin. Leave a child without a diaper and it will soon smear its fæces over everything – into its eyes and even its mouth. I can't imagine how many mothers have come into a room and found their babies covered with shit.

'Shit,' he repeated, liking the sound of the word. 'We pack it into tins and label it cadmium yellow, gentian violet, lamp black.' To Robert's alarm, he squeezed a ribbon of ochre into his palm and proceeded to smear it in a great wet patch across his bare stomach. '– We can't leave it alone. It has for us an undying fascination. And why not? It's the first and primary art! But – this is the point.' He clapped a fist into a palm. *'It belongs where it belongs!* – Not on canvas. Don't mistake the dung-heap for the flower that it nourishes. *That's* what they have forgotten. They plaster our walls with pure dung – and because we are dung-lovers ourselves, we applaud.'

'My glasses,' Robert murmured weakly.

'You left them over here,' Eduard said, and returned them covered with paint, impossible to wear.

'So you don't like my painting!' – He wheeled, and stared at it drunkenly – the colossus on his wall. It seemed acres long, miles high.

'What's wrong with it?' he demanded sullenly. 'I know! It offends you – because I didn't paint it with my arse.' He tried to focus his eyes and finally picked out Robert's pale and unhappy face.

'Well, it's true,' he added, his head bobbing like a buoy in rippled water. 'I didn't paint it with my arse. I painted it with *this.'*

And the astonishing man grabbed a handful of paint-smeared trousers between his legs.

Aghast, Robert tried to rise for a second time, but was again restrained – this time by a huge ochre-wet paw.

For the moment, he couldn't resist or compete. Confronted with this kind of vulgarity, he was impotent and mute.

Yet employment of such language – and such outrageous behaviour – even if the man was drunk! – constituted a great weakness in his opinion, a sign that an animal had been trapped – it was cornered and beginning to snap viciously but with innocuous teeth.

He glanced down at his shoulder. His shirt was ruined – covered with thick ochre paint. This, more than anything, angered and irritated him.

'I merely ventured to suggest,' he said, rising abruptly and moving quickly out of Eduard's reach, 'that the painting's physical *size* was a mistake.'

'And I venture to suggest,' Eduard replied with a slight formal bow and in the fanciest tone his drunkenness would permit, '– that you go take a flying fuck for yourself.'

But his tone had changed; the arrogance, the authority was edged with doubt. He had stopped his weaving, and seemed partially sobered. Robert seized the opportunity cruelly.

'If your painting were as big as my palm,' he said loudly, shouting a little – as if he were in a noisy classroom calling his students to order –'it still would have been tremendous – and you could have painted it in a day instead of a month.'

Eduard stared at him stupidly while the writer added, softening his voice to a conversational level: '– Have you ever seen photos of Henry Moore's work? A figure of his sometimes appears as tall as the Colossus of Rhodes, but then you discover under the photo that the actual work is perhaps ten or twelve inches high.' His eyes moved to the painting – the yards of sweat and toil. '– Think of the work you could have saved yourself; the time.'

'I have all the time in the world,' Eduard murmured sullenly.

'No one has enough,' Robert returned, keeping his ground. 'Particularly the artist. It is his deadliest enemy. So it must be used wisely – and to its fullest. Your mistake here is essentially intellectual. You failed to keep in mind the painting's statement – which has no relation to its physical size.'

146

'What is its statement?' Eduard asked, his voice a school-boy's.

Robert shrugged, and paced a little. 'Simply: the sea is infinite: infinitely beautiful, infinitely mysterious. And——' since he was being completely truthful and honest '– you have captured that – admirably. Your composition is magnificent; your colour breath-taking. But – you have forgotten "the world in a grain of sand" – and sought to *sensationalise* your statement, and thus cheapened it. You bludgeon your spectator with overpowering size, consequently the statement itself becomes secondary. Looking at your painting, I must fight off my astonishment at the artist's audacity in tackling anything *quite* so large *before* I can even begin to see what the painting says. You present your own energy and ambition as the subject instead of *what* you are painting. Of course——' he shrugged '– if that was your aim, then I must say I'm impressed. On the other hand, if your wish was to communicate your statement – to me, since I am, let us say – representative – then I must advise you that you have wasted your time.'

That was it. Rounded, whole, moral, complete. Robert felt better. The nervousness was gone. And he no longer cared about his ruined shirt.

The artist's reply was as cheap, as sensational, as absurd as the size of his painting.

'And what do *you* do with your time?' he inquired, sobriety leaving him in a flash. '*I* know you. I meet you everywhere I turn. You're not a man, you're a sponge . . . a cultural amœba, and your fundamental process is "taking in". Female: your law is female: encompass, engulf, absorb, swallow up . . . that's your law. When you do "give out" it's to tear down, reduce to minutiæ anything that has expansiveness and grandeur. My friend——' Eduard grabbed up a brush and shook it under Robert's nose '– for all

147

your knowledge, all your precious intellect, the very secret of life has escaped you: and that is "to enlarge, to thrust forward and into, to penetrate".' He snapped the brush in half. 'But you! – you must examine pitiful details, criticise, pick over, dissect, destroy any largeness that you find. And do you know why? – because it's a threat to you – a deadly threat – it reminds you of your own – *convoluted* smallness!'

With that Eduard opened the studio door. There he stood – a half-naked savage, covered with sweat and war paint, at least a pint of *obala* burning the lining from his stomach.

And Robert, his nervousness back in full force, filled with rage at the paint on his shirt and the fantastic disorder of the afternoon – walked politely out. When he got to the bottom of the stairs, he heard the door close with a resounding crash.

3

It was impossible to move, impossible for Mildred to turn her glazed, unblinking eyes from the hideous thing!

The *valdepeñas!* The astonishing flower consisted wholly of a double rounded ovary at the apex of its stem and, crowning this, as thick around as her wrist, gently curved, the colour of pale, muddied gold, a giant style!

Membrum virilis! – no other association was possible – proud, erect, glistening wetly in the sun, so ghastly that the hair at the back of her neck began to rise.

She stood paralysed before it, crawling with horrified pleasure, the cold sweat on her forehead an instant haze of shining beads.

Was *this* what she had waited so long and patiently to see? – this – this horticultural monster! – this gleaming incredible pistil with its round and bulging stigma, more living flesh than plant to the eye!

And what to the touch? – But she would not, could not feel it, and each damp hand clasped the other tightly behind her back; while her heart pounded and her thin blouse wilted to her damp body.

In her periphery vision, the world moved by her on either side. A *buedera* passed on the road above the church ruin – the lame one from the hotel, straw sticking from its mouth.

Minutes later, Corbodéra's old black crow swooped overhead, squawking hoarsely, dropping a large red berry that landed at her feet.

Still later, the Constable's child, Evangelina, wheeled by

149

on her bicycle. She carried a bunch of bright flowers and wore a starched *penora*. Mildred hadn't the strength, the mind, to return the child's shy greeting.

Only the *valdepeñas* existed; only its irresistible flower: nodding heavily now, alive and trembling in the sudden hot wind that, like a sigh, rose from Corbodéra's hot and sighing sea.

4

W HEN Mildred didn't appear for two days, Mrs Carter
decided it must be the labyrinth of her inner ear. The poor
child remained virtually incommunicado, but occasionally,
if one rang persistently, would answer her phone.

'Shall I send up some soup?' Mrs Carter asked, connected at last. She shouted the words because Mildred's ear
trouble usually made her a little deaf.

'How *kind* of you!' Mildred replied, her voice so faint
and flower-soft that Mrs Carter imagined she was connected with another planet. '– But I don't want anything.
You *know* how I am. – Just to rest. I must keep my head
still to level the fluid . . . and that's why I don't answer
the phone. By tomorrow, I'll be all right. I know I shall.
I'll be fine.'

And she was. Somewhat pale; more irritable and moody
than ever, impossible to be with for long; but physically,
at least, she appeared rested and refreshed.

'Truly, you must have levelled the fluid,' Mrs Carter
said. 'You look fine. *Much* better.' She lifted her nose,
sniffing delicately. 'Is that a new perfume you're wearing?
It's an exquisite scent.'

'I'm not wearing perfume,' Mildred replied sullenly.

Now why should the child trouble to deny it? Actually
she reeked of it: a mixed flower scent, and not at all
artificial. The room, with Mildred in it, seemed filled with
living plants: jasmine, perhaps; mixed with lilac and violet
and rose.

5

'. . . I HAVE known poverty and ignorance all my life,' Gia went on. 'These last few years I have known wealth; but still ignorance. The rich – and for that matter, the talented – are not much different from the poor. – A rare few, perhaps. They live only to grab, and the things worth grabbing are two: money – and sexuality in one form or another. – Usually another.' She smiled, thinking of Roberto Razizi. '. . . So these considerations of the mind, as you call them, have been new and exciting to me. I begin to see the world as richer than I thought. But through it all——' she paused, hesitating '– I remain a woman. And I do not understand.'

Astonishingly, Robert had no reply. He had been staring at the sea while she spoke, and now he continued to stare.

'Signor,' Gia implored, the word in her use being more intimate than his name, 'for the first time in years I feel myself blushing. . . .'

And still Robert stared.

She covered her mouth with the tips of her fingers; then, taking them away: 'Surely I am not wrong – about you, about me!'

Robert cleared his throat, turning to her briefly, almost casually, but when he spoke his voice was strange, and his eyes stranger still. 'I'm not – certain I know what you mean.'

'We are too much friends for that,' Gia replied, her eyes clouded. 'How well you *do* know!' She had an impulse to hold his chin, keeping his eyes to hers. '– We walk, we talk, we read, we swim. . . . And not once, not once in all these weeks have you touched me, not so much as held my hand. . . .'

Robert wetted a ring on his finger, dried it against a palm; cracked a knuckle, and then another, while Gia senselessly removed several things from her beach bag and replaced them quite as senselessly. This done, she simply stared at him – at his profile, the back of his head – all that was available to her.

'Signor,' she said finally, her voice beginning to edge itself with cold, 'I do not *need* a man. Certainly not as painfully, as desperately, as you need a woman.' She paused, a touch of her gentleness returning. '– Or is it . . . is it that women – *bother* you when it comes to that?'

He did not seem to be breathing properly. The chin was high, the mouth partly open – as if the air were too thin, and painfully dry.

'I'm sorry,' he murmured abruptly. 'Give me . . . just a moment.'

'Ten moments,' Gia exploded, relieved to hear him speak. 'Twenty – a thousand! We are friends.'

Robert's smile was quick and weak, but it was a smile. He lifted his eyes to hers for a moment and then returned them to the sand and the sea. 'Somehow, with me,' he said, 'there was never time – for that sort of thing.'

The axis on which the world turned seemed to be 'that sort of thing' but here was a man who had no time. Gia scratched her nose.

'– Or,' he went on, '– for that matter – most of my life, there was never any particular, never any – *great* desire. – Oh, *sometimes*! – but nothing . . . unmanageable; nothing I couldn't handle. – Alone.'

Well *that* was a confession. He suffered from it and reminded Gia of nothing so much as a discovered boy, agonised and shamed.

'So?' – She inquired with a shrug. Her own auto-eroticism while it lasted had been touched with genius: there was nothing she had not used, or thought of using. But the final dismal truth was that nothing would truly do. Nothing less than a man.

'The idea,' Robert said, 'of being – dependent on another person . . . to satisfy one's needs, to afford . . . "relief" – such an ugly word! – or even pleasure, was always intolerable to me.' He picked up a handful of sand and let it drain through his fist like the grains in an hourglass. '– I simply crowded it out of my life. I didn't seem to *need* it, actually. I didn't look for it.'

'But it looks for *you*,' Gia said, surprised; 'it greets you on every corner, nods to you from every window. It is hard to see how you could hide. Or would want to. Surely sometimes there was someone who was right.'

'There was too much to think about,' Robert replied; 'too much to do. I was always . . . so busy; my life was too full.' His voice, to himself, seemed uncertain and weak. He made deliberate effort to strengthen it. '– There was my work; there was art. That can be a great fullness. The mind, the intellect – the aesthetic sensibilities – give more pleasure, subtler pleasure than the body.'

'But that is to separate this into that and that into this,' Gia replied with sudden impatience, her voice touched with passion. 'Signor, I know about work – and I know about art – and they both come from here' – she placed both hands flat on her lower torso '– not from here——' she tapped her head. 'It is all one. *En tor cardo feora!* – Art! – If I stand before a great painting, do I "admire" it, do I "appreciate" it? – signor, let us not quibble. I *sleep* with

154

the artist: he is there on his canvas – his eyes, his hands, his body.'

Her easy passion, her characteristic naturalness, her wide, expansive gestures depressed Robert even more. He sat crushed and small before her, his hands clasped tightly, his gaze so low his eyes appeared to be closed.

And Gia's astonishment grew. This man! – who more often than not made the schoolteacher cover her ears or run off and hide – who would have put Rabelais to shame with his parade of ribald humour, his sexualised wit – was little more than a façade. It seemed that even Roberto Razizi had not taught her the important lesson: that the mind could grow, even the talent mature, while the heart remained a frightened child. Was this another baby to rock in her arms? – this . . . *doctor* of philosophy. He could explain the theory of relativity so simply that even she with her weak brain began to feel a little the excitement of understanding, but he could not reach forward to kiss her cheek or hold her hand – though he obviously wanted to so desperately that desire was a white sickness on his face.

She looked at him and waited, but waiting was no good. Her body ached with pity, sensations of humour – and all the affection, curiosity and – yes, desire, that had grown through weeks of being with this strange man.

'It is too sad!' she cried, almost laughing. 'Signor, I cannot bear it! Look: you are afraid; very afraid. Of what I do not know. Perhaps you do not know. Nor do I care, since what you fear is in you, certainly not in me. Believe me, I could not hurt you if I tried. – And if you will permit me – if you will *allow* it to happen – I will prove it to you. Will you take my advice?'

'What is that?' Robert inquired, lifting his head.

'– You will come to bed with me – now. This instant. I

insist. Immediately. Come——' She took his hand. 'We will go back to the hotel. We will *sneak* into my room.' She laughed. 'The bed is wide, the sheets are cool. We will lie quietly, still. Nothing will be forced. You will look into my eyes, and see that they are gentle; then, if you want to, you will place your hand – so, on my heart; you will feel it beat. . . .'

Robert's cold, damp hand rested in hers, his brow a maze of wrinkles, his eyes round and panicked.

'There's . . . nothing . . . I want more,' he said. 'Nothing. But . . .'

'Yes?'

'– If you would give me – a little time. To quiet myself. To prepare.'

'That is not the way,' Gia replied. 'That is to think; to plan, to make up things that are never there.' She released his hand, tapping her head. 'That is the brain again. You must answer what is here——' and she flattened her hand over her heart.

'Tonight,' Robert promised whitely. 'Or tomorrow, perhaps.'

6

IN Paris and New York, in Buenos Aires and West Berlin, in twenty great cities simultaneously, this woman's incredible, voluptuous body moved across the cinemascopic screens of the world.

Thousands of men were sweating. Others were sitting paralysed in their seats, generating so much saliva that they had to swallow continuously. Even the boys who were lacquered and perfumed – even they were dreaming that they could . . . well, *almost* sleep with that marvellous body . . .

– So thought Eduard Poussard, lying drowsy and relaxed on the beach beside the fabulous Italian beauty.

They had lunched together, walked the deserted shore – the only ones hardy or foolish enough to stand the afternoon's open heat, the disturbing stillness, the strange surf-less swell of Corbodéra's now dark and oily sea.

Gia Imola, Eduard thought: the international shock to the senses. – The fantasy-body materialised. – The eternal ghost of the eternal dreams of dozing men. – Perfect. Incomparable. Flawless.

'I have an itch on my back,' she said, grunting a little. 'Would you scratch it?'

He opened his eyes and touched his fingers to the back that was a multi-million-dollar corporation.

'– No, no; to the left; down a few inches. – There!' And she sighed with relief.

'I am getting tired of Corbodéra,' she murmured as he scratched. 'I may leave sooner than I planned. I am restless. – Perhaps it is the heat. Usually, I do not mind. I have sweated every summer all my life. I have stewed in that hothouse which is Rome.' She glanced over her shoulder at Eduard. 'I can afford air conditioning. I have much money. In Hollywood, they are renting me a house with a swimming pool. My agent tells me it plays underwater music.'

'Is that better?' Eduard asked.

'Better? – It is better than swimming under water *without* music. It is a wealthy, it is a *rich* thing to do.'

'No – I mean your back.'

'Oh. Yes; thank you. – I shall swim to Mozart. How do you like that! Or perhaps I shall find some cool music. Debussy. He is full of cool music.' She dried her forehead and cheeks with a bit of white tissue and settled back on the blanket, her shoulder touching Eduard's. '– When I was a girl, on hot evenings I used to sit out on the Piazza del Giaveno – the one near Lecco – do you know it?'

Eduard shook his head. '– I have not spent much time in Rome.'

'– Well, no matter. It is a cheap place to go. The wine is cheap. And one has to sit out in the open if one is alone. To sit near the trees is death. Every evening someone is dragged off into the darkness and raped.' She paused. 'But the music I enjoyed. It was the most beautiful thing in the whole of Rome for me. . . .'

She was silent; her eyes fluttered closed, and Eduard watched her.

– A fabulous body! So perfect it seemed unreal, impossible for any man to own, to possess. It belonged on the screen. Besides – a stupid woman, really. Yes, in some ways a very stupid woman. And a stupid woman never loved well. She substituted an avalanche of flesh for spirit. She had no sense of time, or timelessness – no humour, no play, no rest.

But – a fabulous body! Impossible to paint. No one would believe it. On canvas it would look cheap, and exaggerated. Laughable. – The breasts – marvellous! – the glory of God! – but like two perfect, impossible melons.

He laughed.

'What is it?' Gia inquired, opening an eye. 'What is funny?'

'Nothing,' Eduard replied. '– A private thought.'

. . . Once, in a sun-drenched field of France he had used the ripe warm flesh of a melon. He had thought of it since as his 'first affair' – better in some ways, much better, than the stupid, agonised time he'd had with his first girl that very same summer. At least the melon didn't weep and wail and demand that he live with it for the rest of his life!

Had it come to a choice, he would gladly have married the melon. Certainly he'd never touched one since without a twinge of excitement in his groin! – and that was more than could be said about many women he had known.

'You are having too many private thoughts,' Gia complained petulantly. 'Your mouth is twitching and moving: you are laughing with yourself. I am jealous.'

'I'm sorry,' Eduard said, this time laughing aloud. 'I was thinking of – my painting.'

'– Ah. "The Sea of Corbodéra".' She sat up, drying her face which was once more glistening with sweat. 'It is good you did not paint it now' – glancing toward the water. 'Look – like oil. I keep puzzling. . . . Perhaps a tanker exploded.'

'Ten thousand tankers,' Eduard supplied.

'– Then Robert is right.'

159

'Why? What does he say?'

'Something – geological. Or – I've forgotten the word. – To do with the sun. A sun-spot; only another name. Something.'

Eduard brooded momentarily, his finger patterning a circle in the sand.

'He did not like my painting.'

'Robert? I am surprised! – Then he is a fool in that respect. Perhaps he has envy. *I* have never *seen* such a painting.'

'You *did* like it! Tell me – what quality – quickly now – don't stop to think – what quality about it impressed you the most?'

Gia's hesitation was only slight.

'Its tremendous . . . size,' she said. 'I could not look at it – *so*: in one piece; I had to turn my head left and right, up and down. Signor, it is like my films: you are painting in cinemascope!'

She couldn't have said anything worse. His sensitive face was an instant mask.

'What have I said! – Signor, I am sorry. But is cinemascope so bad? People will flock to see your painting – to look – amazed – because there is so much of it! In my own case, the demand is so great that my second film will be released in *three* languages: yes.'

He was still glowering in his beard.

'Signor; I *said* I was sorry. In a way, you are insulting me as much. Is cinemascope to be despised? Are films so grossly inferior to paintings? – I have seen some vile paintings in my time.'

Eduard made an effort to clear his face.

'You are right,' he said. 'And I'm sure your films will make many people happy. They will be entertained – and that is important. But your comparison was not apt. It's like calling *crêpes suzette* and roast pig the same – simply because they have a common characteristic – they are both foods.'

'I see.' Gia nodded thoughtfully. 'You have made it clear to me. – I am not very bright. Brightness is not a big thing with me. But I am loving and honest; and I have a good heart. That is one thing I have, signor.'

'And that is all that really matters,' Eduard replied. He was disarmed, but it still took some effort to smile. He relaxed now, his hands beneath his head, his eyes on Corbodéra's sultry, almost sulphurous sky.

'So you are not very bright,' he repeated, and, slyly, '– But surely you were graduated with honours.'

'Honours?' Gia questioned, confused.

'Yes. I refer to the "Robert Hunter" university.'

Gia was unexpectedly embarrassed.

'Oh!' she said. 'I see you have *not* forgiven me.'

Eduard laughed. 'I have. Truly. I am joking. – And curious.'

'He is a sweet sad man,' Gia sighed.

'You're not friends any longer?' he inquired. 'Your – relationship has cooled?'

Gia hesitated. 'We are the same. It is just . . . he is busy now. And this heat. He is back at work on his book. That is why he came to Corbodéra.' She was anxious to speak of anything else. '– About your painting, signor; if you do not mind. . . .'

'Yes?'

'I am puzzled by one thing.'

'And what is that?'

'How will you get it out of the room? – Off the island? It will be worse than moving a piano.'

He *was* right. She was a stupid woman.

'Despite its size,' Eduard said, 'it's not thickly painted.

And it is not stretched. I simply take it off the wall and roll it up.'

Gia was astonished. 'I see!' She thought about this. 'And then what? Where will you take it?'

'Oh – to Paris, or perhaps New York.'

'Yes? And then——'

'I will exhibit it, of course! "The Sea of Corbodéra"! I don't paint entirely for my own pleasure. What I have, what I do, must be shown. I have exhibited many times – in many countries.'

'– You will not find a gallery big enough to fit it.'

'Then I shall cut it in twenty pieces,' Eduard said, almost harshly. 'I shall sell it by the yard. – "The *Seas* of Corbodéra"!'

Gia was silent.

'You are depressed,' she said presently. 'And I understand. I am like you. When I finish a film, all the life in me is gone. And I think – ah, I am spent, finished, done. I am empty, and I have failed. But it is because we give so much. We give *all* when we work. . . . But afterwards, in a week or two, a month perhaps, life is fresh, new – and we are ready to begin all over again – seeking to find, to show, to express the thing we thought had eluded us the last time. Signor, *we* are the lucky ones.'

And Eduard thought: perhaps she is not so stupid, after all.

'Tell me,' he said, 'more about Hollywood. And the pool that plays music.'

7

Nothing she had ever experienced, nothing in the whole of her long and crowded life, had ever irritated Mrs Carter more than the disappearance of the *valdepeñas* flower.

The moment she heard that it was missing – that some wretched, sneaky person had actually taken, *purloined* the blossom – she seemed to step out of character entirely. Instead of the lovable mild manners that were thought completely her nature, she exhibited behaviour so hostile, irritable and extreme, that the others, with the exception of Mildred who seemed quite stunned by the theft, retreated in shocked, tiptoe silence to their rooms.

For a long while, poor Señor Gutiérrez, who had been summoned post-haste to the hotel, had to bear the burden of her attack.

'You should have posted a guard,' she upbraided him shrilly. 'The *valdepeñas* should have been watched, every minute of the day and night. Señor – you have failed miserably in your duties. So miserably, in fact, that it is not beyond consideration that I shall find it necessary to post a letter to the authorities on the mainland about you, and report in detail on the deplorable status of law on the island. The Constabulary of Corbodéra is not to be taken lightly, you know; it requires a person of experience and integrity; someone who takes his duties seriously. . . .'

'But señora——' the Constable twisted his greasy, sweat-soiled cap in his hands '– the *valdepeñas* was not among my duties. I can prove it. I have papers. I have many complicated brochures, in fact, which list in detail the specific duties of the Constabulary. . . .'

'There is duty by implication,' Mrs Carter reminded him severely. 'The law, above all, must be interpreted correctly. Any comprehensive application would include, as your first and primary duty, the full protection of Corbodéra's citizens and guests. Can you deny that? But look what has happened! I am ill-protected; my whole sense of security has been shattered; I feel quite unsafe, in imminent danger. . . .'

'Danger?' Miguel inquired timidly. '– From what, señora, if I may ask?'

Mrs Carter paralysed the man with a cold, steady stare.

'Constable Miguel Gutiérrez,' she said slowly, 'a thief who steals my money or my jewels does not bother me – beyond the material loss involved, but the thief who steals from me a flower! . . .'

The Constable's shoulders moved in a small involuntary shrug. It was clear he would never understand the subtleties of spiritual crime.

'Perhaps a bird . . .' he offered hopefully, with a glance at Mildred. 'Perhaps Pablo Gonzales . . .'

'Who?' Mrs Carter inquired sharply.

Miguel smiled sheepishly. 'That is Corbodéra's old crow; that is what we call him. He lives on the island each summer. Surely you have seen him.'

'Indeed I have,' Mrs Carter replied. 'I have often fed him from my balcony.' She turned to Mildred, forgetting her purpose momentarily. '– And I have discovered that he likes cashew nuts and cheese – which I must say . . .' But she would *not* be diverted. 'What has Pablo Gonzales to do with the *valdepeñas*?' she asked of the Constable.

'He is a big thief,' Miguel replied. 'He will steal any-

thing. He has pulled the ribbons from my daughter's hair
– when they are red or yellow.'

'I want him followed,' Mrs Carter said instantly. 'You
must follow him and find his lair.'

Miguel's mouth hung open. 'Señora – it is impossible!
Pablo Gonzales has wings. He goes up and up – gliding on
the wind, high into the mountain behind the hotel.'

'You will find a way,' Mrs Carter insisted unreasonably.
'You will take the *buedera*.'

'The *buedera*!' Miguel held his head between his hands.
'She is a cripple! It would take me – *three* days . . . to go
half the way!'

'Nevertheless . . .'

'Señora, I beg of you. . . .'

Mrs Carter glanced at Mildred, hoping for a word of
encouragement and support, but the girl was silent, her
eyes downcast.

'– It *is* a silly idea, isn't it?' she sighed, defeated now, and
sank into a chair looking at the Constable. '– By the time
you got there, the flower would be dead – it would be
nothing: a few dried petals. You didn't think of that, did
you!'

'No, señora.' He was relieved and anxious to leave. 'But
it is true. – And we do not even know that Pablo Gonzales
was the thief.'

'I sincerely doubt it,' Mrs Carter returned, her anger
growing once more. 'The idea is preposterous! The thief
was human, you can be sure of that. – Oh, when I think
of it! . . .'

Again she paced the floor, while the Constable, smiling
and obsequious, bowed his way backward through the door.

8

THE tide was full at dawn, and like a silent army, disciplined, exact, the things that are carried by the sea, but seldom to Corbodéra, washed silently to shore.

A cantaloup from Venice, perfectly round and full, its flesh intact. From America, a rust-stained condom that some sad and sandy lovers had used upon the shore, a milk container, the tube from a neon lamp. A gin bottle from Portugal, a skein of rotted fishnet from close-by Spain. Bottle caps, onions, a broken oar.

And the things that belong to the sea: the back of a spider crab, opalescent, a saucer cut from the sky; shrimps in their dying the colour of melted butter, green weed like knotted hair.

And washed in by the sea was a legless kitchen chair, its wood swollen and black, scarred with clusters of luminous barnacles.

It was caught by the crest of a wave and in a majestic sweep was spun to shore. It washed out again, then in, blistered with yellow foam, caught itself on a rock, and settled slowly, perfectly erect, on the sand.

There it waited. A king could sit in such a chair; or a clown.

Part Five

I

On three successive evenings, Robert approached Gia's suite, and on three successive evenings suffered a paralysis that rendered every muscle in his body useless except those of his legs which, when the time came to lift his hand and rap on her door, carried him promptly away.

He'd returned to his room, so stung with embarrassment and shame, so loathing himself and the tyranny of his body that a full pint of *obala* was the measure of his pain.

On the fourth evening, he reversed the process, consumed the full pint of *obala*, spread his mind wide to the full range of his sexual imagery, and so equipped and aroused, issued the dim and drunken orders that carried his body up the winding stairs to her door.

There, the usual tyranny took over.

There was lust in his chest, in his eyes, in his hands; it crowded his throat and his lungs, but the place where it belonged was a desert where no living thing grew.

He must have made a sound; perhaps he groaned, or sighed, or even breathed too heavily – because the door opened suddenly and there was Gia; wet from a shower, an immense blue towel wrapped about her, the smile on her face fading gradually as she confronted the pale, sweat-drenched corpse at her door.

One puzzled word: 'Signor——' and the rest was a pantomime.

She opened the door wide, and he advanced into the room as a man condemned to prison might for the first time examine the cell where he is to spend the rest of his

169

life. This done, he sat by the window, his back to her: small and hunched, both hands tightened between his knees.

Behind him there was no sound: she was standing still, watching him. Then, after a long while, he heard her move slowly across the room, the heels of her mules kicking lightly against the polished stone floor. The room's light was dimmed suddenly, a sheet rustled as she threw it aside, the towel sighed as it dropped from her body, and then the ancient bed groaned as it supported her weight.

He watched Corbodéra's full moon drifting grandly above the sea.

Next he found a small golden figure on the beach – Nicky no doubt – and followed its winding path along the moon-wet shore.

The stars interested him; the great blue stain of the *ptonisoris* leaves below Gia's window.

So his life, or his death, was delayed.

'Signor?——' Again a single word: helpful, gentle, edged with hesitant humour; puzzled, kind.

He rose and turned and looked at her. It was quite too much to bear.

2

'. . . But the child in us never dies,' Paul said. 'It is indestructible. Our tragedy consists in our attempt to kill it. The result at best – or at worst – is of course repression. We succeed in burying the child – alive.'

'Goodness!' Mrs Carter exclaimed with an aghast look. She had a vision of a child awake and breathing in its coffin, interred under six feet of earth. '– Each of us, then, is his own murderer. We are *all* infanticidal! – did you know that?' – and she now looked at Mildred, trying to draw that morose child into the conversation. The girl had been silent and depressed for hours – and the mood had persisted all week. Even her knitting held no interest, though she carried it with her, keeping it in a tangled heap by her side.

'I do suppose I must have read it somewhere,' Mildred replied meanly. She smoothed her bathing suit across the stomach. The gesture was slow, rather lingering, and it was a gesture that Mrs Carter had observed often within the last day or two, and one that startled her each time because it seemed so very much like the unconscious gesture of a pregnant woman.

'Well,' she said, since Mildred obviously wasn't to be cheered, 'at least the universality of it is comforting. I do rather like the idea of mankind's *general* neurosis – I mean, our all being in the same boat, so to speak. The private neurosis can be embarrassing, and so often lonely. But to have one – that everyone else has . . . well, at least it's cosy.'

171

Paul laughed in his winsome but irritating way. He never took what she said with the proper degree of sobriety.

She added defensively: 'Well, one doesn't have to *lock* oneself in one's room, does one? One can be neurotic and very well *in* things. – I am certainly glad I am not privately neurotic. It is difficult enough to work on the general neurosis without having to bother about that.'

Gia, as usual, had been straining to follow the intricacies of the conversation, her forehead a relief map of concentration.

'About what?' she demanded with a baffled look.

'The private neurosis, of course,' Mrs Carter replied. She scolded good-naturedly: 'Now *do* pay attention; it isn't often that we can induce Paul to talk shop.'

'But I don't understand,' Gia persisted. She removed her reading glasses from her beach bag and placed them on her nose, as if clearer vision would improve her capacity to understand. '– Why do we suppress the child at all; why——'

'*Re*-press,' Mrs Carter hissed helpfully.

It was obvious Gia didn't know the difference.

'It is done *to* us,' Mrs Carter explained. 'It happens *in* us but we don't know it's happening. It's like – well, a toothache; we make our own tooth ache – certainly no one else does, but we aren't responsible, so to speak. *It* does it; in the case of the repression, the unconscious.'

'Ah, I see,' Gia said, though it was doubtful that she did. 'Then let me ask this: *why* does it happen? Why does the unconscious do this thing? *Must* our children be buried? I say they should live!'

'And I agree!' Mrs Carter exclaimed with éclat. 'Let the child live! – Endlessly, totally – all our lives. I vote for a veritable Garden of Eden – the perpetual innocence and delight of infancy! Why not?'

'The theory,' Paul replied, 'and I paraphrase Freud——'
he inclined his head slightly in Mildred's direction '– is
that opposed to pleasure is reality: the world is real, the
world is hard; there is survival, there is work, necessity –
a culture that demands the sacrifice and exists only because
that sacrifice is made. What would a world of physically
mature polymorphous perverse adults be like? Could such
a world exist at all? Wouldn't we play away time in
infantile pleasures? Civilisation would be a sand castle, a
mud pie on the beach. . . .'

'Unless,' Mrs Carter interrupted, 'work itself became
play.'

Paul smiled at her warmly but a bit teasingly. 'If you
have the secret, you must tell me. And everyone else. The
world is waiting to hear.'

'Well, I don't imagine there's any *real* secret,' Mrs Carter
replied. 'It's simply a matter of doing what you enjoy, and
enjoying what you do.' She was suddenly sad. 'I enjoy most
everything I do – and yet I do nothing. Nothing *important*,
that is. But this winter I intend to change things. Truly.
What I have in mind . . .' She stopped herself. 'But I will
tell you that later. Some other time. We were discussing
play – and children. Mildred's forte, I might add,' and
she waited hopefully. This time she was rewarded.

'Have you ever *watched* children play?' the girl asked
with at least a semblance of life. 'Their play is senseless and
disorganised. It is only when they are *instructed* or begin
to emulate their adults that their play acquires any meaning or purpose.'

'But play *has* no "purpose",' Mrs Carter replied, happy
that Mildred had joined the fracas, 'unless you want to call
it *organic*, or *visceral*. What is the meaning of enjoyment?
It is meaning itself. What you are proposing, apparently,
is that children's play without mature guidance is entropic.'

'I certainly am,' Mildred replied, 'though I would hardly choose that word. – Leave a classroom of children to itself and in ten seconds flat there's bedlam – a roomful of screaming, dancing idiots. There's nothing closer to a mad-house. I sometimes think that all children are mad, and that the task of education is simply to rear them to sanity.'

'Sanity,' Mrs Carter questioned archly, 'being the general neurosis we were speaking of? Oh – it *is* a problem I do admit. But you are being just a bit unfair. In school, the atmosphere, even in so-called play, is one of restriction and suppression; no wonder children exhibit a few wild excesses once you leave them to themselves. Goodness!——' her eyes rolled heavenward '– when I think of all those *nervous* games we called "play" – spelling bees, and musical chairs. Can you think of anything more fraught with anxiety than musical chairs? – everyone rushing around in a dizzy circle, and then the horror of not finding a chair of your own – of being cast out, rejected! It's no wonder we're all neurotic! Even the games we teach our children are based on the severest kind of aggression and competition. – But take *free* play – the play of the very little child, or made-up play away from school . . . the co-operative, imaginative kind: spontaneous, relaxed and, heaven knows, *not* organised . . . this I *do* maintain is negatively entropic – in a deep, perhaps biological sense.' She paused reflectively. 'I have heard, you know, that evolution-wise we are all descended from a gibbon-type animal, a small, lively creature, understand – not at all aggressive or competitive, but characterised by its gentleness, intense curiosity and above all its desire to prank and play. . . .'

Mildred was depressed again and stopped listening. These endless 'intellectual' conversations which used to amuse and, in a way, instruct her, now seemed in themselves 'play' – the play of adults, as pointless, disorganised

and meaningless as the play of children. She found herself wanting to join the conversation only when she was
angry and had something sharp and bitter to say. The
others had grown sensitive to this and no longer asked for
her opinions – with the exception of Marion. And Marion
asked anyone's opinion – even Nicky's. 'The young are
closer to God. . . .' It began that way.

She was still talking, and now gesturing so energetically
that there seemed no part of her ample anatomy that wasn't
part of her flowing verbiage.

'. . . Nor do I quite believe,' she was saying, 'in all this
strange business about culture – its being "nothing but" a
sublimation of our repressed infantile longings. There is
something wrong somewhere, and all these clever people
with their "nothing but" philosophies had better think
things through again. Why there isn't a field of endeavour
– no art, not another science, that the psychoanalysts aren't
poking their fingers into, and sniffing and mouthing so
about it that one might well inquire into the anality and
orality of that! To read the current literature, one would
think that a telescope is "nothing but" a tremendous
phallus *penetrating* the heavenly "bodies" in sublimated
incestuous intercourse. But who has psychoanalysed psycho-
analysis, may I ask? – and yet it is one of our supreme
cultural achievements, *the* supreme one I dare say. Consequently, it must be "nothing but" a sublimation of our
repressed infantile polymorphous perversity. – Yet it pro-
poses to save us from the very thing to which it owes its
own existence. Now I call that biting the hand that feeds
you – indeed, a veritable serpent's tooth. . . .'

3

To Gia without Robert beside her, a whispering interpreter, Paul and Mildred and Mrs Carter – sometimes Victoria if she troubled to stay awake – talked in a foreign tongue.

She rose quietly from the sand, taking Nicky's hand, and stepped carefully over the Countess's gently snoring body. They waded.

The sea was warm. '– As hot as minestrone,' Gia said, splashing a little. She kicked a pale, half-grown onion out of the water. '– And as *full* as minestrone. When one has to swim with an onion, it is time to leave.'

'Something is going to happen to this island,' Nicky said darkly. 'I keep dreaming about it.' He wiped the sweat from under his nose.

'Like what?' Gia asked.

'I don't know. – Exactly. But something pretty bad.'

'Like what?' Gia persisted.

'Well – Like an earthquake. Or an avalanche. Maybe a tidal wave.'

'Is that what you dream?'

'No. But I'm always in the water; it swirls me round and round; like in a whirlpool. And everything is steaming; there are big sounds, like thunder. – And I am going down, down, down.' He said it cheerfully, squatting by degrees to illustrate.

'And you dream this often?'

'Yes. All the time.' He scratched his brown hairless chest. '– At least five times already.'

Gia thought for a moment, her eyebrows raised, while she dried the moisture from under her nose.

'Then I would advise you to stay out of the water. You should not swim alone.' She was quite serious. 'Listen: I have a little sister who dreams. Lucretia. If she dreams of blood, I will not touch a knife. If she dreams of lightning, I stay indoors when the storm breaks. I have *learned*, believe me. – I am taking her to Hollywood with me, so I will know what to do and what not to do.'

'But I'm real good now,' Nicky said. 'I swim as good as Eduard.'

Gia shook her head. 'No; no you should not swim alone. Not with such a dream. Did you tell the Countess?'

'Who?' It was his supreme stupidity that to this day he didn't know who the 'Countess' was.

'*Victoria!*' – No one could be patient forever.

'Oh. No; she worries about things like that; she might make us leave the island.'

'– I think we should all leave.' She glanced about, first at the dark oily sea, and then back at the hotel, the chalk cliffs behind it, vague in their veil of yellow mist. 'We keep waiting for the beautiful weather, but it never comes. All we get——' she kicked at the insolent vegetable at her foot '– is onions. And there! – beets.' There were two, like twins. She picked one up, pressing it into his hand. 'Here – give *this* to your Countess – bortsch!' At his bewilderment she laughed. '– Do you see! It gets worse and worse. Yes, tomorrow I will wire my manager. I will have him start to *arrange* things. – My departure. It takes a great deal of arranging, you know. The Press must be notified.'

'Who?' Nicky inquired. He was a baseball pitcher, winding his arm in a great swinging arc.

'The Press. They are the newspaper people.'

'Oh.' The beet flew from his hand, making a phosphorescent splash in the sea. Even the sound was oily. 'Did you see that! Did you see that curve!'

Gia nodded, finding a flat rock to sit on. 'It is necessary that I be photographed. It is very important. – Everywhere. – At all times. Arriving, departing, sitting on trunks, stepping off planes, signing autographs, not signing autographs. . . . And I say things, too. That must be decided. Nothing is left to chance.'

'What do you say?' He sat beside her, but on the sand, fingering the claw of a crab he had found.

'Well – I don't know. Not yet. No one has told me. It must be discussed with my manager. Perhaps I will give my opinion of American men – that is usual.' She frowned. 'Perhaps *too* usual. Everyone must be tired of hearing what Italian stars think about American men.'

'What *do* you think about them? – American men.'

'I don't think about them at all.'

Nicky opened the crab's claw, aiming it at her foot.

'Suppose you were swimming,' he said, 'and this gigantic crab came along, like this.' He closed the claw gently on one of her big toes. 'It could really bite; it could make you bleed.'

'So I would bleed,' Gia said. '– Perhaps I should discuss American *women*. How different they are from the European. I'll have my manager think of something shocking to say. – That is necessary. Whatever you say, it must be shocking. Otherwise no one knows you are there – and all the arriving and departing has been for nothing.'

'Then what?' Nicky asked. 'What after that?'

'Then – nothing. I am there. I am arrived. I have shocked everyone; I have been photographed in a gown that reaches to here——' she showed him '– and I am working on an American picture. – With a big American star.'

'I'll miss you,' Nicky said sadly, resting his head on her knee.

Gia smiled, stroking his sun-streaked hair.

'Perhaps I *do* think about American men after all. – They are gentle, and sweet——' she lifted his chin '– and very, *very* beautiful.'

'– *Oh!*' With his usual embarrassment at any reference to his beauty, Nicky pulled away.

Gia turned to glance back at the others. Mildred had left, and Suzette had joined her husband. Victoria was still asleep and Marion still talking, her hands moving in wide, inclusive gestures.

'Are children entropetic,' Gia asked Nicky, 'and if so, what polyamorous repressive is the result?'

'What?' he asked.

She shrugged, a sour look on her face. 'Beets and onions and boys I understand.' She took his hand. 'Come. Let us find a *geistata* nest and crack it open. I will understand flies, too.'

'But you can't,' Nicky laughed, rising quickly. 'The nests – they're hard as steel. Harder. I got a sledge hammer from Señor Gutiérrez and hit one with all my might. No one can open them.'

'The *geistata* do,' Gia replied. 'All the little *geistatas* fly out in the spring.'

4

'WHAT I don't understand,' Victoria said, 'is how *you* can bear it. Tell me. – It's because you are so thin, I suppose. There's so little to you.'

'I sweat, too,' Nicky murmured.

'I sweat, too!' she mimicked good-naturedly. 'But you also run and jump and swim and play as if it were twenty degrees outside. Do you know it's one hundred and two? – Yes. Nicky, let us leave. Tomorrow. Señor Gutiérrez will tap his little wireless and in the morning the plane will be here.'

Nicky's smile was quick and brave – and thoroughly artificial.

'Okay,' he said brightly.

'Okay, okay,' Victoria echoed. 'But you want to stay with all your heart. Don't lie to me, Nicky – even with a smile. It is too warm for lies. No one should lie when the temperature is one hundred and two.'

Nicky lowered his gaze.

'Is it Eduard?' Victoria inquired. – A frown and no reply. 'But he is making eyes at the actress. Isn't it so? He has no time left . . . for boys.'

Nicky lifted his eyes, blazing, and Victoria's white teeth caught at her underlip.

'I'm sorry,' she said. 'I am wicked. There is no lie worse than a half-truth.'

She sighed, adding suddenly: 'Very well; we will stay on Corbodéra.'

She had turned quickly and was just in time to see it

at its purest: the full radiance of Nicky's smile. It was a
flower that opened before her eyes, breaking her heart and
healing it, all in one moment. For such a smile, such a
look, she would have stayed if the temperature were two
hundred and two.

Ah, that boy! How pity had grown. It had been his
grief, his illness in the beginning. That he was 'human' – a
boy – made little difference. So she would have nursed back
to health a dying bird she had found in the Roman streets,
and lavished it with a care that was passion. But now——

'Nicky?'

He walked quietly to the chair by the window, thinking
it was time for the sitting.

'No,' Victoria said. 'We will not sit today. It is too hot
– even for looking. Let us talk just a bit. Then you can
go back to your artist, or your swim, whatever you choose.'

Nicky nodded, surprised; it was the first day in months
they had skipped a sitting. Uncertain, he stood in the
centre of the room.

'Here,' Victoria said, patting the gold settee. 'Beside me.
– I have business in London – after we leave Corbodéra.
Then, I thought, we would go to America. – To the
"States", as you say. To Brooklyn. I want to speak to your
uncles.'

Nicky didn't move or speak. One eye twitched nervously.

'I have only one uncle,' he said presently.

'– Well, to him then. – What is his name? – I have forgotten.'

'It's Joseph.'

'Ah yes. Passanante. Your father's brother.'

'Yes.' He sucked on a finger as if he had pricked it with
a thorn.

'Look at me, Nicky. Let the finger go. Aren't you
curious?'

'About what?'

'About why I want to see your uncle, of course.'

Nicky swallowed and blinked.

'I'm not – curious,' he replied. 'I know. You want to see him to explain. To tell about – my mother, and Rome – and how sick I was, and the papers being lost, and Corbodéra.'

Victoria nodded. 'Yes. In part. Don't you think that should be done? Isn't it necessary?'

Nicky hesitated; then shrugged. 'I suppose. – You don't know my uncle.'

'Of course I don't know him. That is why I'm going.'

'I mean – he never bothered with us none. I never saw him hardly. I don't think——' Nothing more. – A tight, still boy, his shoulders hunched, picking at his fingers.

'– You don't want to go back to America? – Nicky, speak to me. It's very important.'

'I don't know.'

'But you must know! You have feelings. What do they say? What do they tell you?'

Nicky took a deep breath. 'Since you ask——' he began shyly, and then blurted: 'I want to stay on Corbodéra. Or go back to Rome.'

That strange, sad look was beginning to come into Victoria's eyes.

'Why?' she asked. 'And I want the truth – from the heart. Tell me what you *feel* – don't think.'

'Well——' he *was* thinking '– it's nice here; the island is pretty. And Rome . . .'

'Pretty! The island is pretty!' she moaned, turning a wild, pained face away from his.

His panic was instant and overwhelming.

'*Don't do that!*' he shouted, terror ringing his voice like a bell. 'It's *you*! I want to stay with *you*!' – touching her chin with fingers that trembled, turning her face, her eyes back to his.

Victoria went limp; for a moment he thought she had fainted.

He was on his feet, his whole body shaking. 'I'll get you some water. You need water.' And, echoing Robert Hunter's favourite phrase, 'It's this *damnable* heat!'

5

'I HAVE always considered Mildred a rather plain young woman,' Suzette said. 'But now she is rather beautiful. She is relaxed and peaceful. She is doing her hair in a new soft way. Even her skin has changed; it is clear, transparent.'

It was a question, and Paul did his best to answer it.

'Pregnancy does that to some women – apparently even the kind she has.'

. . . Maas into the windup . . . the pitch . . . swung on and missed. Strike one . . .

It was the sudden blare of Nicky's radio. Suzette closed the louvres in the door to their suite.

'What?' she asked.

'I said – apparently even Mildred's kind of pregnancy can do that to a woman.'

Suzette looked at him oddly. 'You're sure she *isn't* pregnant?'

Paul was astonished.

'You've seen her! She looks six months pregnant – in six days' time!'

'I know,' Suzette pondered. 'But – suppose, just *suppose*, it's true. I mean – that it's God as she says . . .'

'Suzette!'

'– Well it *has* happened before. How can you be sure, absolutely sure?' And she seemed almost to mean it.

' "To repeat", as Picasso says, "is spiritual death",' Paul tried to joke. 'I expect God to be infinitely imaginative – and resourceful.' He was suddenly gloomy. 'We joke. God help

184

us, there *is* something funny about so many of the psychoses – the *irrational* factor – like in so much of our wit. – During the war we had one soldier who was obsessed with the idea that he was turning into a roman candle.'

Suzette began to laugh, covering her mouth with her fingers.

'I agree – it *is* funny,' Paul said; 'and it was the prize joke at the hospital, too – until one day the boy got out into the motor pool, doused his head with gasoline and set fire to his hair. He was burned blind.'

Suzette stopped laughing, her eyes wide with pity.

It was stifling with the louvres closed; Paul opened them.

. . . Mantle is getting under it . . . he's got it! . . . one away . . .

'Poor Mildred,' Suzette whispered. She felt giddy and sick, and wanted both to laugh and cry.

. . . Minnie Minoso, the batter . . .

6

' "My love is like a red, red rose . . ." ' Eduard said in the moonlight. 'Do you see? – an image helps, a figure of speech, but to attempt to define love logically is rather like trying to explain a colour, or the odour of perfume. It's impossible.'

And Gia agreed, kicking off her shoes to wet her toes.

'We keep forgetting,' Eduard continued, his fingers laced through hers, 'that words are symbols, mere signs pointing to or representing an experience. That is why I paint. For a while when I was young I thought I would write, but two years at it convinced me that words, at their best, are too far removed from life – from living; they leave one with a feeling of emptiness and loss – of unreality. You write – and what have you? – a million scrawls on a thousand sheets of paper. To experience what you have written, to understand what you have said – if you have said anything at all – the reader must go one-two-three through time: connect word after word like beads on a string – for hours, perhaps for days. But a painting is total, instant in its experience; the viewer can see simultaneously everything you have said – a million cumulative brush-strokes – a month's or a year's work in one beautiful, complete moment. There is no dreary one-two-three, no dribble of symbols through the mind and its distractions before one can begin to feel and appreciate what you have done.'

Gia nodded. 'But painting,' she observed wisely, pulling her skirt above her knees and splashing a little, 'must have its dreary side, too – from the artist's viewpoint, since to do what he has done he must go, as you say, one-two-three himself.' The intelligence of her own mind was astonishing her this evening. It was not so difficult to talk philosophy after all – at least with Eduard.

'That is true,' he replied. 'But the process – the work for the artist involves a kind of true living in itself; it isn't all in the head and scratching with the fingers or pecking at typewriter keys; one is *body*-involved; there is the paint to deal with, the expanse of the canvas; one uses one's muscles; the breathing is deep, the heart pumping, one moves back and forth, in and out of created space: it is as real as dancing.'

'I see,' Gia said. 'It is closer to my own art; to acting.' She paused thoughtfully. 'But to return to love . . .'

'Love is a poem,' Eduard supplied, laughing. He touched her fingers to his cheek. 'Love is a drunkenness and a dream. . . .'

'Love,' Robert echoed in the distance, his voice rather faint, 'is an old douche-bag hanging on a bathroom door.'

Eduard strained his eyes toward the rocks on the left, making out the writer's silhouette against the moon-washed sand. Robert had shifted his position for the third time, but had been sitting near them for a good half-hour, plainly eavesdropping and commenting like a Greek chorus whenever something they said interested him.

'What *is* the matter with that man?' Eduard asked, lowering his voice. 'Why does he keep annoying us? – By God, everyone is losing his mind!'

Gia placed a restraining hand on his arm as he stood. 'No. Let him be. He is drunk, and very angry with me – though I do not care. Let him take his foolish revenge.'

'Let's leave then,' Eduard suggested. 'We'll walk on down the beach. Look – it's almost as bright as day.'

'It would be useless,' Gia replied. 'He'd only follow us. He has been following me all day.'

'Well, I'll certainly put a stop to that,' Eduard said, quite loudly.

'Don't bother,' Robert called. 'I'm going. I'm *bored* with this cheap movie romance.' He rose and walked a few steps away, then turned, his drunken voice shaken in his strained effort to keep it careless. '– But I must warn you that the stones are mossy. – And wet. I suggest you move higher up on the beach; by the sea wall preferably. But *there* I must caution you against the sand.' He paused, adding softly: '– A sandy coitus can discourage the most *sublime* of passions.'

With that he moved on. They heard his footsteps on the stones grow faint.

There was an awkwardness between Gia and Eduard, a silence and a waiting.

Presently Gia asked curiously: '*What* was that word he used?'

Eduard scratched his beard.

'Coitus?' he asked gently.

Gia nodded.

'It means,' the artist replied, looking at her, '. . . to fuck.'

Gia's tongue touched the inside of one cheek thoughtfully.

'Ah. – So,' she said.

'And you know *that* word?'

Her beautiful profile, silhouetted by the moon, inclined itself gravely.

'I have . . . encountered it,' she said. 'It is written on the walls of Rome.'

7

THE moonlight was bright enough; fluid and glowing, it splashed its mixed silver and gold across the sand, but Gia and Eduard had moved to the far side of the ruined sea wall. They stood head and shoulders above it, arms and bodies locked, so distorted and grotesque with shadow that they seemed like two ghastly puppets performing on a stage. In the next moment they had dropped from sight.

With a weeping oath, Robert threw his binoculars aside and began to crawl through the spiked biting leaves of the *ptonisoris* plants, across layers of sun-dried weed and salt grass, circling the wall, toward the lovers on the sand.

When he got close enough to see dimly, he moved on his belly as soundlessly as a soldier into an enemy camp.

Now they were plain, and he closed his throat to the crowding nausea that seized it, while with streaming eyes he watched the two moon-washed bodies in their fantastic postures of love. His eyes could bear it, but not his ears. The sounds of love were unendurable. With a stifled cry, he curled upon himself like a foetus, spewing forth his sickness into the recesses of his own folded body.

8

HAD a heel or a pale green tendril touched the wall of its tender prison?

Divine babe! Flower Prince!

Mildred had to leave off her knitting, her hands trembling and crippled – straining consciousness away from the tide of drowsy ecstasy that would drown her.

For in her, she knew, God had united, in a glorious mutation, two great kingdoms of the earth.

She was the instrument, blessed and pure, who would give birth to the second Adam, the neo-Christ who would populate the world with a new and beautiful race, half human, half fragrant lovely flower.

– Religiously tropistic: turning to God as to the light!

– Green blood: streaming corpuscles of chlorophyl!

Feet! hands! or occasional hearts rooting in the gentle earth to drain the clear, cold elements.

Conception spiritualised; sublime. – Pollen; living clouds of sparkling dust enveloping honey-wet styles arched bold and clear in the sunlight!

And oh, the scent! – drenching the world with mixed lilac, jasmine, mimosa, rose. . . .

9

'Why did you tell Paul Dier about me?' Mrs Carter asked, her face drawn and pale. 'I have been kind to you, Robert, very kind. I thought we were friends. I loved you – as a friend loves a friend.'

Outside, the sky was darkening, filling his room with the strange green shadows that had come to Corbodéra. And in the eerie light that was so watered and sea-like, his face was thin and haggard, gleaming with sweat. On the floor was a half-filled bottle of *obala*, another on a chair. There were two crates under the window. The rest of the room was a shambles.

'What did I tell him?' he asked faintly, seizing the back of a chair.

'– That I am an ambassador's daughter,' Marion replied; 'that my father was a suicide.' It was painful and embarrassing to look at him. '– That I have never travelled, never married, but lived the whole of my life in Spain – coming only as far as Corbodéra each summer to be near my father's grave.'

Robert turned away from her; then, hurtfully, so insultingly: 'A psychiatrist inspires confidences. He can't be much of a psychiatrist if he told you what I said.'

'He did not tell me,' Mrs Carter replied, the pain alive and pressing in her chest. 'He told his wife – and by accident I overheard. I am not a patient of his; if he repeated it to Suzette it's quite natural, and I understand. I don't reproach him. But *you*——'

'I said nothing that was not true,' Robert murmured, his

voice now hoarse. He turned to look at her, narrowing his eyes until they were direct and deliberate, almost evil in their desire to hurt.

'You *are* an ambassador's daughter. Your father *was* a suicide. You *have* lived all of your life in Spain.'

Mrs Carter's eyes fluttered closed for a moment as she mouthed a few silent words.

'Truth,' she said finally, her voice shaken and low, 'is not a physical event. Not to me. Is memory more true than imagination? – the sight in your eyes more real than the dream in your heart? Robert——'

She had to stop because the astonishing man was suddenly on his knees before her, begging forgiveness, his crying the kind children know, so passionate and wild that she could do nothing but stand helplessly by until the sounds from his throat had diminished to a series of broken groans and coughs, audible swallows of mucus and tears.

He was finally still, and as if nothing had happened stretched himself back on the floor, his hands beneath his head, his wet red eyes focused on the ceiling.

Mrs Carter seated herself in a chair by the window, staring at him, and was silent for a long while.

'You have worked,' she said presently. 'You have worked well this summer. I have heard your machines tapping away at all hours of the night.'

'Shall I tell you what I have written?' Robert asked dully.

'I would like to hear; I would very much like to hear.'

He rolled to one side, pointing to a thick yellow manuscript lying on his table.

'How shall I describe it?' He thought for a moment, adding with a sly, strange laugh: 'What you see is a tome that consists mainly of the most minutely detailed descriptions of the sexual anatomy and physiology of the human male and female bodies in every conceivable state of rest and arousal, of the imagined psycho-physical pleasures of a fantastically conceptualised sexual intercourse. In short, it is a religion of sexuality, a ream of pornography so clinical and detailed that it would curl your hair where you sit should you read the very first page.'

This was indeed surprising and bewildering news.

'If it is comic . . .' she ventured, not quite understanding. 'After all, there *are* publishers who . . .'

She paused, ashamed of her own stupidity.

'I see,' she said quietly.

She was silent, looking at him stretched out on the floor, so shockingly thin, his clothes wrinkled and soiled; he had been living and sleeping in them for weeks.

'I know of many men, *many* fine men who have been——' she shrugged slightly, '– *rejected* as suitors and thought the world had come to an end. Why I once had a friend – *years* ago – who actually . . .'

It was clear she had missed her mark. Apparently, it was the other way around, and being so, was so very much more serious. He had failed where, to him, failure was fatal.

'I see,' she said again, and breathed deeply. '– So what is to be done? If you are going to kill yourself, there are quicker, more interesting ways to die. I am surprised and disappointed that you should have chosen *obala*.' She smiled at him sadly. 'Tonight there will be a full moon; I suggest you swim out to sea: straight out, stroke after stroke, until you are completely exhausted, and cannot lift your arms at all. . . .'

Was it senseless to try to pique him?

'– Shall I sit here for a while – quietly? Do you want to be with me like you were with your mother? – lying on the floor with your bottle?'

His answer was a long noisy sucking. He gulped at the *obala* greedily, delighting that it spilled over his chin, soaking his chest.

'What is the difference,' he asked wetly, 'between a bottle and a grave?'

10

The Countess knew it was Nicky – even at that vast distance. Why else was she here? – on the beach before dawn, her heart pounding, her cheeks wet with tears, probing like a ferret among the fantastic débris the night had piled on the shore.

Crowned with a clown's cap of seaweed, he was half-sitting, half-reclining in a legless kitchen chair, his head flung backward and awry as if the neck were broken.

Beside him, around him, the sea had flung up its museum: a crescent of melon bled of its colour, a tar-black orange, the reaching open-fingered forearm of a celluloid doll; rotting starfish, molluscs, a headless fish.

The king had been interred with his treasures, the clown with his joys.

With a cry so pierced with anguish that God must have covered His ears, Victoria dropped to her knees, sprawling in the garbage, seizing it in wild rooted handfuls, flinging it in every direction to make a clear, clean place on the sand where her dead boy could lie.

I I

THERE was not a bruise on his body, but the sea had stained him with its colour; his eyes were open the widest she had ever seen, the child's sweet genitalia curled in a blue shrivelled knot between his legs.

She seemed cut out of stone beside the body of her love, the cold small hands in hers.

'I wanted nothing,' she said, 'nothing but to look at this child.' And now she knelt on the sand and with imploring gestures denied her guilt to the others who, in Corbodéra's pale and fluid dawn, were grouped in a ghostly tableau around her.

'– I would not have kept him; only for this summer. Truly; that was my plan. And I did not try to change him. I did not dare even that much. You could *see* his vulgarity. Surely you noticed his clothes. I gave him money – that is all – and he bought his own. And his haircuts – how dreadful they were! He ate what he liked – hot dogs and coke. I only worried him when his skin broke out – that is the only time I ever spoke – and insisted he eat vegetables and fruit. I loved him, but left my arms open. Come – go; stay – leave; he was free; that is the way it was. I chose him, to begin with, because he would be impossible to own; it would be folly to even try. But now – do you see what has happened?' She rose, grey and trembling, to her feet, beating senselessly at the air. 'God will give us nothing! – even when we ask so little.'

Mrs Carter came forward with a moan, her groping hands outstretched, giving what little comfort there was to give. She locked the Countess in her arms, opening her heart to share the heartbreak.

'– Only to look,' Victoria went on, her voice bleeding in the dawn, 'that's all I ever wanted – to fill my eyes with his exquisite face. Is that so much? – *he* didn't think so: he came to me gladly, freely every day – and sat by the window. He watched the sea, and the fishermen, the little boats. Is that so difficult? – We rarely spoke. What could we possibly say to each other? What *is* there to say that the eyes will not do – if the eyes are honest and unafraid? There is more meaning in a look than in all the philosophies you can name.'

And now her voice shattered. With strange, inchoate cries, she emptied her strangled passion into Mrs Carter's arms.

12

EDUARD remained with the boy while the others, with tender arms and tear-wet kisses, led the inconsolable Victoria away. Then he knelt on the sand, the breath leaving his body in a bursting sigh. For a moment, in the wildest of hopes, he considered pressing his mouth to the boy's, breathing his own surging life into the body; but there was now a bruised blackness on Nicky's lips, the head twisting so sharply when he touched it that it was plain that the neck had been cleanly broken.

What does one do with one's beloved dead?

'Forgive me,' he whispered, weeping.

He pressed the cold curled fingers to his lips, then, done with it, rose, the frail body in his arms so light it seemed like nothing so much as a flower.

Part Six

I

CORBODÉRA's first tremor was so slight that those who felt it at all, introjected it, imagining themselves touched with vertigo.

Corbodéra's second tremor was severe.

In the Polonaise dining-room, Mrs Carter sat aghast, her nose covered with jam, watching the tea service bounce and clatter across the table, two cups crashing to the floor at her feet.

She wasn't sure when it started whether it was actually the island or a poltergeist, but when the chair beneath her began jumping like a pogo-stick, careening crazily across the room, she knew it was Corbodéra.

Before her eyes, the pink plaster wall on the sea side of the hotel split down the middle in an instant forked fissure. It was so like a stroke of lightning that she waited breathlessly, almost expecting to hear a resounding crack of thunder.

There was no thunder, no sound at all for several moments: only a fantastic motion beneath her, rather like a sudden dizzy drop in an elevator. Then, after a final jolting shudder, the island became still.

Surely it had burst every pipe in the hotel! She could hear it distinctly – but was it the plumbing? – like a thousand drowsy bees: the murmur, the bubble, the rush of distant water.

2

'I CANNOT find the room clerk,' Mrs Carter said. 'Nor the *maître de*. They have *all* deserted; I cannot find anyone – only the *buedera*, and he is tied to a palm tree in the lobby. – I suppose someone thought he would be safer there.'

'Where is Señor Gutiérrez?' Eduard demanded. 'Where is the wagon for my painting?'

They were all quite peevish.

'He has gone,' Mrs Carter replied. 'He was worried about his daughter.'

'Well, he had better worry about us,' Eduard said threateningly.

'He is a disagreeable man,' Gia contributed. 'He is lazy and careless and not to be depended on in a crisis.'

'We are *all* aware of the Constable's shortcomings,' Mrs Carter agreed patiently. 'But that is neither here nor there. The point is – I sincerely doubt that he will be back – with or without his wagon.'

'But he *must* come back,' Paul said abruptly. 'How are we to reach Tanique?'

'I'm afraid we cannot,' Mrs Carter replied. 'It's quite impossible.' She looked from one to the other in embarrassment as if she were personally responsible for the frightening rise of Corbodéra's tide. '– Look!' – and she lifted her skirt, showing them her legs, wet to the knees. 'That is from the lobby. And you can see——' she gestured to the rising lake in the garden below '– what is happening out *there*!'

3

THE Diers, who had several times made courageous if fool-hardy attempts to leave the Polonaise, now sat stunned and astonished amid the remains of their sea-soaked luggage, Suzette holding her wilted hatbox, and Paul his camera and two wet books, both of them by Freud.

Twice, after it seemed certain that Señor Gutiérrez would not return with the wagon for their belongings, they had tried to walk, indeed, to wade to Tanique where they futilely dreamed they'd be rescued, only to turn back less than a quarter-mile from the hotel, stopped by an impass-able fissure in the road through which the sea boiled and churned in a rolling river.

Eduard, whose only concern was his painting, had rolled it into a nine-foot package, and sat with the immense bulk of it across his knees. He was pale with rage and clung to the canvas so protectively that it might have been his wife – or a beloved child.

Gia did nothing but stare stupidly at the sea.

'What is happening?' she asked monotonously, going from one to the other. The 'what' that was happening was happening before her eyes, so no one troubled to explain.

'It will pass,' Paul said with startled brightness, his eyes on the unbelievable sulphur of the sky.

There was hope, not belief, in his voice.

4

HADN'T everyone *known* what would finally happen to Corbodéra? Hadn't each been told or warned by the other – or himself dreamed or fantasied the island's death?

The Countess didn't care.

Jewelless, devoid of make-up, her body sheathed in the blackest black her wardrobe would provide, a cloud of sombre tulle scrolled across her face and hair, she sat, a black and soulless queen on the veranda of the Polonaise, watching the water rise.

That her boy had been washed from the sea like a tarred orange had been evil enough. To have found him sitting on a legless kitchen chair – this touch had killed her. No one could bear it. No one. So the battle was over.

Mildred, her body ripe and blown to a fine full round-ness, was quietly serene. She was comfortably, calmly seated in a beach chair not far from the Countess, knitting a pair of booties for the future king. What was there to fear? – The sea, creeping inch by inch up the Polonaise steps?

'What an unnatural tide,' she commented placidly.

Her body would be an ark in the flood; of this she was certain, for she still bore unborn within her the flower-prince of the new world, the saviour-king.

Robert seemed to care even less than the Countess. His death was being sucked from a bottle. He had been drunk for two weeks, and in two weeks' time had lost so much weight that he appeared half his size, the eyes enormous, the cheeks hollowed.

He sat astride the balustrade like a boy on his rocking horse, the hotel's last crate of *obala* cached protectively between his knees.

Gia still could not assess the significance of the sea's rise, nor the self-evident magnitude of its threat, even though Mrs Carter reminded her several times of the ichthyologist and what he had told her.

'But he said it would happen *thousands* of years from now,' she protested, taking it all as a shocking inconvenience and only vaguely remembering Marion's long rambling story of what would one day happen to Corbodéra.

Mrs Carter shrugged helplessly. 'Have you a better explanation? The sea isn't *rising*. The island is obviously *sinking*. Surely you feel it. Every few minutes there is a definite *drop*.' She turned inquiringly to Eduard and the Diers. 'You *do* feel it.'

Suzette nodded – rather dazedly Mrs Carter thought, though in the circumstances it was quite understandable. The water had reached the very top of the Polonaise steps and was now beginning to ooze through the flagstone terrace in the most alarming way. Paul was too busy to answer her, or perhaps even to listen. He was quite the most practical of them all, and for two hours now, with Eduard's help, had been piling into groups and tying together all the gilded chairs the dining salon would supply.

'There will be two of us to a raft,' he said as the work progressed.

They were indeed peculiar rafts – each a huge porcupine of red plush and gold leg sticks. It seemed unlikely that they could keep anyone afloat for long, but Mrs Carter thought it best not to criticise. She restricted her comments to words of encouragement and praise.

'– Mildred, you and the Countess will share one,' she

said. 'Paul and Suzette. Gia and Eduard. That leaves . . .'

'I'm not going,' the Countess announced through her cloud of black tulle. They were the first words she had spoken all day, and had the eerie, disembodied quality of a medium's control.

She had no sooner said this when Mildred, who was trailing a languid hand in the water by her beach chair, refused a raft, too. 'I shan't need it,' she said mysteriously and in so other-worldly a tone that the others were silent, wearing their mortality like threadbare cloaks, except for Paul who, splashing through the knee-deep water, turned on her savagely.

'I'm not going to insist,' he shouted angrily. 'I'm not going to *beg* you – any of you – to try to save yourselves. Go, stay, live, die – do as you damn please! It seems unlikely that *any* of us will survive, but I for one, and my wife with me, are going to try.'

'Hush, Paul; hush,' Suzette whispered, wading to his side to draw him away.

She was awed by Mildred. Whether it was insanity or saintliness burning in those eyes, the light was unmistakably there.

Unnoticed, Robert had passed out, sliding silently from the balustrade into the water. A current caught him, and he would have floated past Mildred and directly out to sea if she hadn't the presence of mind to catch at his belt and hold on firmly until Eduard, with an oath, came to her side to drag the man from the water.

5

'I HAD a great aunt,' Mrs Carter said, clinging to her raft, 'who wanted very much to die in her sleep.'

– Certainly the subject was apropos, and they were all far too adult to employ euphemisms or to pretend that they wouldn't most certainly die.

'– Penelope; that was her name, though we children always called her Aunt Penny. Do you know what she used to say? "– When my time comes, I hope I go in my sleep." She was always saying that. And she did! – Go in her sleep, that is. She went to bed one night and simply didn't wake up the next day.'

Holding tightly to their own raft, Paul and Suzette were making love; at least they were kissing each other, very gently, like two small children.

'– I remember my mother telling us: "Your dear aunt's time came last night, and she is gone." Of course, we were so young that all these references to "coming" and "going" were quite confusing. After all, "to come" and "to go" are very *active* verbs and rather difficult to associate with death.'

Gia and Eduard were fussing with their raft and barely paying attention. The Diers, however, had finally stopped kissing and turned in her direction.

'In any event,' she continued, directing her remarks to them, 'after Aunt Penny *had* gone, we were all brought in to see her. Actually! It was the fashion those days to expose children to death at a very early age – if anyone *did* die, that is, and it does seem to me that people died much oftener then. Of course, families were larger – and I suppose that is the reason. Goodness! – We were always being dressed up in our party dresses to view some second or third cousin who had died. Why we got so used to it after a while that it was impossible to put on our long faces and act at all solemn-like. Why I remember——'

6

PAUL had nothing to say about death, nothing at all it
seemed, though Mrs Carter kept looking at him inquiringly.

'Now you're sorry you're not a Buddhist,' she teased,
unable to resist; '– or at least a Catholic. How comforting
that would be! – To know that this is not the end. Tell
me – what did Freud have to say about death?'

Paul hesitated. '– A great many things,' he replied; 'none
of them particularly applicable at the moment.'

'He did not believe in survival?'

'No.'

'And you do not?'

Paul glanced at his wife, and then away.

'No.'

'You believe there is nothing?'

He shrugged. 'A sleep – a dreamless sleep.'

'That is indeed a possibility, I suppose,' Mrs Carter
agreed thoughtfully. 'But if true, what is there to fear?
Why are we all so pale and frightened; why do we fear
this nothing, this dreamless sleep?'

'I'm sure we don't,' Paul replied. 'Death masquerades;
we fear suffering; we imagine death to be an intolerable
experience. However, death being death, it's not, it can't
be, an experience at all, experience being necessarily con-
fined to that which lives.'

'But we experience *dying*,' Suzette said faintly.

'– Of course. Because dying requires life; it is experience-
able. But at the moment of death, experience ends.'

'Oh that is much too easy,' Mrs Carter exclaimed, motioning to Gia and Eduard to move their raft closer and join the conversation. 'There is something wrong somewhere. I do wish I had read more about death – studied, you know. There must be many books on the subject, aside from the *psychic* ones, a few of which I *have* read. But I was always so busy I never seemed to find time for the more serious themes. That is a mistake, I am convinced. – Now that it is much too late!' And she looked about her dismally, for the water by this time had crept to her waist, the flow increasing to the force of an undertow that was dragging strongly at her feet. She closed her eyes and breathed deeply, praying for strength, for courage, above all for dignity.

'Nevertheless,' she said, opening her eyes, 'I am inclined not to believe in death at all – that is, as something separate and apart from life. And by the same reasoning, I suppose,' she added with a brief laugh, 'I do not believe in life either. – *Per se*, I mean. No – there is neither life nor death; there is life-and-death; an inseparable whole, a synthesis of some kind – like light and shadow, each giving reality to the other. What we call death is *real*; that is your error; it is not a nothingness; it is the shadowed side of life-and-death, just as life is its lighted side. So – although I cannot presume to tell you quite what will happen – when you're dead I mean – I do declare that it *will* happen, and that you will know it and *experience* it, whatever it is. Every change is a dying, and dying the greatest change. You'll see! – All of which seems intuitively self-evident to me; to believe otherwise is absurd – unless you are ill and prefer illusions to reality. . . .'

She glanced toward the Countess who was still seated in her chair.

'Victoria——' she begged, for the water was swirling

about her shoulders, touching the black lace at her throat; 'it is not right; you are making things much more painful for all of us. Won't you please cling to your raft? Come. Do join us.'

The Countess didn't reply. Only a hand rose from the depths of the water to fasten her wet tulle more closely about her face.

'It is hopeless,' Mrs Carter concluded. 'She will be stubborn to the last. I know her.'

At this moment, Mildred, who was as stubborn as, or perhaps merely vying with, the Countess, literally floated from her beach chair despite her efforts to remain calmly seated. Perhaps it was due to the unusual amount of gas in her system, to her pregnancy – whatever the reason, she bobbed like a ball of cork, her rounded belly a half-moon above the surface.

And she was as chagrined as a disappointed child, floundering as helplessly as an overturned turtle, until Paul left his raft and kindly helped her to stand.

'Brace yourself,' he said, his hands on her elbows; 'spread your legs; there's a strong undertow.'

'I'm quite all right,' she answered tersely, smoothing her dripping hair. 'You needn't worry about me.' She added with weighted significance, though its meaning eluded Paul entirely: 'I'm in *very* good hands.'

Nevertheless, she was obviously shaken, and when Paul untied the raft which she was to have shared with the Countess and brought it to her side, she clung firmly to one of the gold legs with both hands.

The glow in her eyes had faded somewhat; her entrails felt chilled, and not for hours now – not since the beginning of the inundation – had she felt any sensation of life within her: not the unfolding of the smallest leaf, not the reach of the tiniest root hair, not the most feathered touch of a tendril. She stared at the dark water swirling about her, then at the fantastic burnt yellow of the sky, and began to pray.

'Now about death——' Mrs Carter pursued – for things seemed settled at last. 'Eduard – what do *you* think? You haven't expressed an opinion at all.'

But again everything had to stop, and the gradual hysteria mounted because Robert, whom they thought securely tied, had slipped from his end of the raft and disappeared.

Paul began immediately to dive, but Eduard was reluctant.

'What in God's name is the use? The man is half-dead already!'

'You *must!*' Mrs Carter cried.

So Eduard dived too, cursing and spitting profusely each time his head rose from the murky water.

The futility of the search was soon evident. Robert was nowhere to be found.

After a long silence, Mildred began to sing – or at least to hum, but she had no ear for music. The most that emerged was a tremulous, tuneless little hymn of some sort.

'Will you please stop it?' Eduard asked.

But Mildred continued perversely, strengthening and firming her voice. Her face was turned to the sky, the eyes rolled in her head like an El Greco saint.

'Mildred!' Mrs Carter begged. She could not bear the smile on the girl's face: the witless grimace that curled her lips in a simpering bow. 'Mildred!' – her voice thinned with horror and heartbreak.

Mildred's pathetic tune, mixed with occasional laughter that was as delighted and delightful as a child's, reached them long after she had gone. Her raft, caught by tangential currents, seemed to weave in a vast circle around them for the longest while.

'Listen!' Mrs Carter whispered several times. 'There! – In that direction! Paul, couldn't you possibly . . .'

But nothing was seen. Only the fog; as yellow and evil as the sky.

7

THE Countess was next, and no one saw her go. Each was too busy with his prayers or his raging or the varied expressions or concealments of his fright.

A scroll of black tulle swept by. There was no need for Mrs Carter even to lift her eyes to know.

8

GIA and Eduard would have lasted longer except for his painting which, so ironically now, Mrs Carter remembered was called 'The Sea of Corbodéra'.

It was tied across one side of their raft like a huge dead fish, and had by now absorbed so much water that it threatened to sink them at any moment.

'You *must* let it go,' Gia raged for the eighth time, this time between bared, clenched teeth.

The raft tilted and she went under, to rise like a gasping phœnix, her hair plastered with weed.

'*Eduard, you son-of-a-bitch!*' She vomited a mouthful of water. '*Eduard!——*'

It seemed for some moments that he would prefer to let Gia go rather than his painting, but finally, and very slowly – his face a gleaming, greenish white – he unbuckled the two belts that held the canvas to the raft.

His painting. It sank with his heart.

– And with unexpected consequences: the raft, relieved of its burden, was propelled to one side so rapidly that both he and Gia lost their grasp.

Had it moved into the relatively still water surrounding the Diers and Mrs Carter, they would have had little trouble. Instead, it spun swiftly seaward, caught in the fringe of a current.

'Come back!' Mrs Carter warned shrilly. 'Come back' – for both were swimming after it.

Gia hesitated, turning her head to glance over her shoulder, but it was much too late.

'*Gia!*' Mrs Carter wailed. '*Eduard!*'

Their heads were two weird buttons sewn to the cloak of the sea.

In the next moment they were gone.

9

Paul's lips were moving silently.

'You're praying!' Mrs Carter accused with an astonished look. 'Now do admit it!'

'Gladly,' Paul replied. '– Though I am neither a convert to religion——' he kissed his wife's cheek '– nor a sudden believer in survival. I am saying the prayers I learned as a child and which my mother taught me. Or rather, they are saying themselves, and hearing them, I find them strangely appropriate and mildly comforting.

'– But I am also a man,' he went on, in a kind of drunken ecstasy, 'and I am praying to God and to nature, to love and to life, to all the energies and desires, the appetites and dreams that perpetuate consciousness aware of itself. . . .'

He had one arm about Suzette and beneath the dark water hugged her fiercely.

They were perhaps minutes from their death, and in those minutes Paul found himself raw with the ache of desire. From his genitals to his heart, his body seemed aflame: searching, probing, seeking, penetrating, reaching for the life he had barely known. It seemed impossible to die. His body denied it; every cell, every drop of his blood. There is no death. No death. Let him drown. Let him decay at the bottom of the sea; his lust and his delight were eternal and indestructible.

Suzette shuddered, her face glistening and pale; he had been crushing the breath from her.

'I'm sorry,' he said, gentle and sobered.

He released her; she drank in the air dizzily for a moment; when the colour had returned to her cheeks, she moved back up against him.

'We're drifting,' she said, alarmed.

Mrs Carter was yards away, and had politely turned her head, permitting them to enjoy what appeared to have been a private moment together.

'My legs are numb,' Suzette added, panicked. 'I have no sensation. I can't kick.'

And neither could Paul.

They struggled futilely to propel themselves toward Mrs Carter, but soon found that they required all their remaining strength merely to cling to their raft.

10

'Good-bye, good-bye,' Mrs Carter called softly, watching the distance between them grow.

Of all the people she had ever known – and there had been so many – surely they were the most pleasant to die with.

'Good-bye, good-bye. . . .'

'Good-bye, Marion.'

'Good-bye,' echoed Paul, so gently.

– So friendly, so warm. Ah, love! – they were veiled with thin fog now; their raft beginning slowly to spin.

'*Auf Wiedersehen*,' Mrs Carter smiled. '*A demain.*'

They were smiling, too! They were both smiling – she could see them!

'I'm sorry the summer turned out so badly' – a tired mother to children falling asleep. 'But I did try to warn you, you know. Surely you will grant me that. I told you about the island. I told you what the ichthyologist said. It is not *my* fault that he miscalculated. And even he is not to blame. It is very difficult work with all those figures, not to mention the various signs.'

She could barely see them now, but it seemed important to go on anyway – just in case, you know.

'– He had one pi too many, I'm afraid. Or' – she had just enough strength left to laugh, '– one pi too few. In any event . . .'